This is no longer
King
D0054323

the
POE
Estate

Also by Polly Shulman

The Wells Bequest

The Grimm Legacy

Enthusiasm

the POE Estate

POLLY SHULMAN

Nancy Paulsen Books · An Imprint of Penguin Group (USA)

NANCY PAULSEN BOOKS
Published by the Penguin Group
Penguin Group (USA) LLC
375 Hudson Street
New York, NY 10014

USA | Canada | UK | Ireland | Australia
New Zealand | India | South Africa | China
penguin.com
A Penguin Random House Company

Library of Congress Cataloging-in-Publication Data
Shulman, Polly.
The Poe Annex / Polly Shulman.
pages cm
Companion book to: The Grimm legacy.
Summary: Sukie braves the twists and turns of the spooky Poe Annex at the New-York Circulating Material Repository to untangle ancient family secrets, find hidden treasure, and help the ghosts who are haunting her house.
[1. Books and reading—Fiction. 2. Supernatural—Fiction. 3. Ghosts—Fiction. 4. Haunted houses—Fiction. 5. Families—Fiction. 6. Buried treasure—Fiction.] I. Title.
PZ7.S559474Po 2015
[Fic]—dc23
2014042105

Printed in the United States of America.
ISBN 978-0-399-16614-3
1 3 5 7 9 10 8 6 4 2

Text set in Bembo.
Nautical illustrations © KeithBishop/Getty Images.
Spooky illustrations © Dzhamiliya Ermakova/Getty Images.
Tree illustrations © darkdaysahead/Getty Images.

To Irene,
a crackerjack agent
and a true friend

CONTENTS

CHAPTER ONE

Cousin Hepzibah

"Almost there," said Dad as we crested the last hill.

The old Thorne Mansion stood black against the sky, bristling with gables and laced with leafless vines. Crows quarreled in the skeletal trees. I couldn't see the ocean, but I smelled its salt. The truck, heavy with everything we owned, lurched and bumped up the steep drive. My new home did not look welcoming.

"It's been a long time," said Mom. "I feel bad I didn't visit more often. Cousin Hepzibah was always so good to my brother."

"Well, you've had a lot on your mind," said Dad. "At least we're here now."

"Come in, child," said Cousin Hepzibah. She was sitting in a wooden chair by the window. Pale daylight slanted down over her, making gray streaks in the air.

I hadn't seen her in years—not since before my sister got sick—but she looked just the same, straight and thin and pale, like a birch tree. She had her white hair pulled back from her face, but her eyebrows were still black. The dark horizontal stripes made her look even more birchlike. Underneath them, her eyes were sky blue.

"You must be Hepzibah," she said. "The one they call Kitty."

"What? No! Kitty is . . ." I couldn't say it.

"Of course," she said after a moment. Despite her age, her voice was strong and low. "Forgive me. I remember now, Kitty is the redhead. You're Susannah—they call you Sukie, don't they?"

I nodded. Did she know Kitty was dead?

Evidently yes, because she went on. "There's always been a Hepzibah in this house, but now it seems I'm the only one living. Come closer so I can see you."

I stepped forward into the gray light. Taking my hand, she studied my face. Her fingers were cold, thin, and hard. They caught me as tight as a blackberry vine when it tangles your sleeve.

"You have the Thorne look," she said. "You favor my aunt Hepzibah. It's good to see her chin again."

"Yes, I look like Mom," I said. "Kitty looked like Dad."

Cousin Hepzibah nodded. "I've given you the tower room. Second door to the left and up the stairs. I would show you myself, but those stairs keep getting steeper. I hope you'll find it comfortable."

"I'm sure I will," I said. "Thank you."

The wind in the branches outside gave a long moan.

"That won't disturb you, will it?" Cousin Hepzibah asked, then shook her head. "No, of course not. Nothing in this house would threaten a Thorne. If you're cold, draw the curtains—the window frames could use some caulking, but the curtains are nice and thick."

"I could fix that," I said. "I've helped Dad lots of times."

Cousin Hepzibah smiled and squeezed my hand. "I'm glad you're here."

When Kitty died, I thought things couldn't get any worse. But they did. Mom had left her job at East Harbor Middle School to take care of Kitty, and she couldn't find a new one—all the schools had hiring freezes. And business was very slow for Dad too.

"Things will pick up in the spring," he said. "They always do."

Except that year they didn't. Nobody wanted new houses built. All Dad could find were small jobs like rebuilding kitchen cabinets so the owners could try to sell their house. Everyone near us was trying to sell their house, but nobody was buying.

The next spring, things didn't pick up either. Mom found a part-time job working at the Easymart, and Dad did whatever small jobs he could. I would hear them talking in the kitchen when they thought I was asleep.

"What if you went back to school for nursing?" asked Dad. "There's always work in health care."

"I don't think I could," said Mom. "It would just remind me, all the time . . ."

I heard Dad's chair scrape as he went over to her. "I know. Sally, Sally, it's okay." They were quiet for a while, but I could tell Mom was crying. "Well, *I* could go to nursing school, then," Dad said. "Lots of men do that now."

"How would we pay for it? The bank's not going to give us another loan."

"No, you're right," said Dad.

I pulled the covers over my head, but it didn't help. I wished I were old enough to get a job. I wished there were something I could do *now*! I helped Mom and Dad with their weekend work, finding interesting old things at garage sales, auctions, and thrift shops to take down to New York City and sell at flea markets. I helped them pack the things up, and sometimes I went along to the city and helped sell them. But it wasn't enough.

The thing is, I was the one who was supposed to die.

Some Thornes live practically forever, like Cousin Hepzibah. Others die young. In my mother's generation it was her youngest brother, George. He died of the Thorne blood disease just before he turned twenty. In my grandfather's generation, it was my great-aunt Caroline and a first cousin of theirs, one of the Hepzibahs.

I was born prematurely, and everyone thought I was the doomed one in our generation. I spent the first two months of my life in the NICU with tubes attached, wearing a tiny knitted hat, which Mom still has.

"You looked like a little baby bird before it gets its feathers," Kitty used to tell me. "I was worried a cat would come and eat you."

"No way you could remember that, Kitty! You were only three."

"Oh, I remember! That's not something you forget. You were so weird and red, with your twig arms and your big, blind kitten eyes. All the time in the hospital, you looked like you were seeing ghosts. Everybody was so worried, and it seemed like forever before they let us bring you home."

I was always small for my age, and I kept getting sick—earaches and strep throat and everything anyone in a three-mile radius came down with. Mom used to make me wear two wool scarves long after the ice melted on the puddles in the backyard. I still had training wheels on my bike a year after I stopped needing them. I wasn't allowed to jump off the diving board by the waterfall, even though all the other kids did it, and forget about swimming in the ocean, even on the few days when it was warm enough.

It was Kitty's job to take care of me. I liked having someone so strong and fearless to stand between me and the barking dogs and rowdy boys. To me, the smell of Kitty's favorite watermelon soap was the smell of comfort. Still, sometimes I envied kids like my best friend, Jess, who was always tearing around without anyone trying to stop her. Mom made Kitty protect me from pretty much anything fun or exciting.

It didn't help that I had the pale, bony Thorne look. I used to slap my cheeks and puff them out, hoping it would make me look more like stocky, rosy Kitty, who took after Dad's family, the O'Dares.

And after all that, Kitty was the one who got the Thorne blood disease and died.

"Oh, here you are," said Mom, knocking on the door frame of the tower bedroom. "Can I come in?"

I nodded.

"I always loved this room," said Mom. "The Round Room, that's what your aunt Jenny called it. It's so high up, with all the windows." She pushed aside the gauzy inner curtains on the four-poster bed and sat down on the end. "Jenny and I used to fight about who got to sleep here. How do you like it?"

I shrugged. "It's fine," I said.

Actually, it wasn't. Nothing was fine, and I was sure nothing would ever be again. Fingers of bare vines—ivy or something—scraped across the windows as if they were picking at a scab. The wind whistled and seeped through the cracks, making the curtains move aimlessly. Cobwebs floated in the air high up where the curved wall met the ceiling. I wanted to go home to my own room in the clean, warm house that Dad had built, the house where I knew all the sounds, where my feet knew every tile and corner. But that was someone else's home now, not mine.

I didn't say any of that, of course—Mom already felt bad enough. But I didn't have to. She came over to the window seat and hugged me. "I know it's a big change," she said. "Things'll look better once you get used to it. We're lucky Cousin Hepzibah has all this space. We're lucky she's so generous."

"Well, it's not like she can live here alone anymore," I said. "She can't even really climb stairs. She needs our help."

"That's right. She's helping us, and we're helping her. We're both lucky," said Mom.

I knew Mom was right. But I still just wanted to go home.

That night I sat up suddenly, absolutely certain there was a ghost in the room.

At first, when I opened my eyes, I thought I might be the ghost myself. The world was as velvety black as it had been with my eyes still shut. Maybe, I thought, I have no eyes. Maybe I have no body at all. But I reached out and touched cloth, which meant I had hands. The cloth was the reason I couldn't see anything. I had pulled both layers of bed curtains closed for warmth, the white gauzy inner ones and the heavy brocade outer ones.

When I parted the curtains, the velvet blackness sank into gray shadows. I had closed the window curtains too, but moonlight seeped through around the edges. A figure was kneeling in the window seat, outlined dimly in moonlight. She had her back to me. The room filled with a sweet smell, like cloves and roses.

I wasn't scared. I was used to ghosts. Well, I was used to one particular ghost, anyway. "Kitty?" I said. "Is that you?"

She didn't move.

"Hepzibah?" I asked.

The ghost turned around slowly. Light glowed softly from her and I could see her face.

She didn't look a thing like Kitty. She looked like me.

I didn't scream. Neither did the ghost. We stared at each other for a few moments. She faded slowly, like fog lifting, until there was nothing in the window but moonlight and shadow.

I pulled the bed curtains closed again, but it was a long time before I fell asleep.

CHAPTER TWO

The Thorne Mansion

Cousin Hepzibah was sitting in the kitchen sipping coffee the next morning when I went downstairs. I almost asked her about the ghost, but Dad was there too, and I never brought up ghosts around my parents. I didn't think they would take it well.

Dad was making his famous cheesy-chive scrambled eggs on the old-fashioned stove. It was weird to have that familiar smell in this strange place.

The kitchen looked nothing like our kitchen at home. It was an enormous room with furniture instead of wall cabinets and tables instead of counters. The floor was paved with slabs of stone. The sink was the size of a bathtub. The stove stood inside a huge fireplace.

"That's an awesome fireplace," I said.

"This is the original kitchen from the eighteenth century," said Cousin Hepzibah. "Back then the hearth was the center of the house, so it needed to be big. Big enough to roast a whole deer in it." She pointed to the spit, an iron scaffold thing in the back of the hearth. It looked like an evil swing set.

"Does anyone ever use it?"

She shook her head. "Not as long as I've been here. In theory you still could. You would have to move the stove and sweep the chimney first, though." She smiled. "Just in case you're planning to bring home a deer."

Dad and his friends did bring home deer meat sometimes, from their hunting trips. It saved grocery money, but I didn't like the strong taste. I went over to where he was cooking and stood in the fireplace squinting up the chimney. It was black and dim.

"Eggs, Sukie-Sue?" Dad handed me a plate.

I looked around helplessly for a fork. Our kitchen stuff was still out in the truck. Cousin Hepzibah pointed to a wooden box on one of the big tables against the wall. I took out a fork with three metal tines and a wooden handle that felt very old.

"Good morning," said Mom, coming into the kitchen. "Mm, cheesy-chives!" She took a plate from Dad, and I handed her a fork.

Mom turned to me. "Dad and I are going to unpack our stuff today, and then we can load up the truck for the flea market in New York tomorrow."

"I want to come too," I said.

"Really? You know how early we have to leave. Wouldn't you rather spend the day settling in? You would be safe here with Cousin Hepzibah."

"No, I want to help."

My parents' weekend trips could be grueling—up way before dawn, unloading heavy boxes from the truck, then sitting at a folding table for hours in the bitter wind or sweltering sun.

But I wasn't ready to stay here in this creepy house with nobody but a cousin I didn't know that well and a ghost.

"Want me to show you the house, Sukie?" offered Cousin Hepzibah. "The ground floor, I mean. You'll have to explore upstairs by yourself. My knees aren't so great anymore."

I followed her out the kitchen door and down the dusty hallway.

In the old days, the Thornes would have employed at least three maids and a manservant, but Cousin Hepzibah had been living alone since her brother died a few years before I was born. She had turned the ground-floor music room into a bedroom when her arthritis got bad. An aide, Alicia, had come in a few times a week to help, but she had to go back to Trinidad a month before we came, after her own mother had a stroke.

Cousin Hepzibah walked slowly, leaning on her cane. Some of the doors swung open with a creak as soon as she touched them; some stuck tight until I thumped them with my shoulder. I'd gotten pretty good at guessing the dates of furniture from helping Mom and Dad with their antiques. Walking through the Thorne Mansion was like walking through history.

The house had started small, only four rooms: the kitchen, the hall behind it, and two little bedrooms above. That part was built in the seventeenth century, Cousin Hepzibah told me. But three centuries of additions had grown like coral—the hollow shells of dead Thornes—burying the original house in encrustations. The Thornes in the eighteenth and nineteenth centuries had made their money from ships. They had added parlors and work rooms, the music room, endless gabled bedrooms, and at the very top, over my bedroom, the widow's walk.

"You should run up and take a look. You'll love the view," said Cousin Hepzibah, pointing up the staircase with her cane.

She was right. Up on the widow's walk, the wind whipped my hair around my ears. I saw the hills and the winding road, the patches of woods, the town and the white church. Far off through the trees I even caught sight of sun on the sea.

A crow landed on the railing and peered at me sideways. I started to lean on the railing, then thought better of it. The paint was flaking off and there were balusters missing; it didn't look steady enough to support my weight. The crow didn't seem worried, but crows have wings. It was getting too cold, and Cousin Hepzibah was waiting. I went back downstairs.

Next, Cousin Hepzibah showed me through the ground floor of the east wing. There, early twentieth-century Thornes had spent some of the money from their investments in railroads and oil on building boudoirs, the gallery, the gun room, the conservatory.

Things fell apart in the 1930s, though. The building stopped during the Great Depression, and apparently the repairs did too. Upstairs, where I went to finish the tour on my own, everything was cold and dusty, festooned with cobwebs. In some rooms, I left footprints in the dust. Clearly almost nobody climbed the stairs anymore.

When I opened the casement window in what looked like a sewing room, I saw Mom and Dad in the driveway unloading our truck. "Sukie! Come down and help," Mom called. I ran down the back staircase, the one meant for servants, creaking the treads.

We stashed our flea market stuff and some of our heavier furniture in the old carriage house, but most of our boxes went straight up into the main attic. It was hard work hauling our things up all those flights. The long, low attic room with its peaked roof stretched over the nineteenth-century additions. Eight dormer windows lit it dimly. A single lightbulb hung in the middle of the room, but nothing happened when I pulled its chain.

"I'll have to fix that," said Dad, putting down his armload of boxes.

The attic had that winter smell of cold dust. Groups of furniture stood around draped with dirty white drop cloths. I felt as if I'd tiptoed into a Halloween surprise party full of little kids dressed as ghosts, holding their breath while they waited to startle the guest of honor.

I added my boxes to Dad's pile and peeked under one of the drop cloths. It covered a collection of wooden chairs with spiky arms and legs. They looked uncomfortable.

"Anything good?" asked Mom.

"Eastlake, I think," I said. "Pretty beat up, though."

Mom looked under a drop cloth near her and found an aluminum and Formica table from the 1950s. She let it fall back.

Something rustled behind me. I spun around. A mouse? A ghost?

It didn't feel like a ghost, and for some reason, I didn't think one would show up with my parents there. I made myself go look. Standing in that corner was a tall mirror in an elaborate wooden frame. My reflection looked elegant and mysterious.

"Now, that's more like it," breathed Mom. "What a beauty!"

"Hands off, Mom. It's all Cousin Hepzibah's," I said. "We can't sell it."

"I know, honey. Can't I admire it?"

"Quit slobbering. You're like a wolf!"

"Don't worry, I'm still a Thorne," said Mom. "Let's cover that."

Together we threw a dusty cloth over the mirror. It unsettled a pile of old leaves by the window—the source of the rustling, maybe. I found an old broom and swept them into a newspaper, then opened the window and shook them out. The wind snatched them away, flinging them up and down and sweeping them toward the sea.

When we were done stowing our boxes in the attic, I took the broom to my tower room. If I got rid of the cobweb trapezes, maybe ghosts wouldn't find the place so hospitable.

The broom felt cold in my cold hands, almost tingly. That happened sometimes—I got a cold, tingly feeling when I touched something, usually something old. I wasn't really surprised to get the tingly feeling in this house, where everything was old.

My ceiling was so tall that even with the broom, I had to stand on a chair to reach the corners. The chair creaked when I stepped on it, and I could almost hear Kitty scolding me to go get a real ladder before I broke my neck.

The chair held my weight. Cobwebs dodged away in the air currents as I slashed at them, and a spider dropped down on a long line to inspect me. "I'm not afraid of you," I told it. "Go find someplace else. This is my room now."

CHAPTER THREE

My Sister's Ghost

When Kitty died, my friends disappeared. Not all at once; Jessica Anthony, my best friend, hung on for a while. Her big sister, Victoria, was Kitty's best friend, so naturally the four of us had spent a lot of time together. Kitty used to say that since she was stuck with me, they might as well bring Jess along too.

Jess and I would make up endless dramas with our dolls. Sometimes they were ancient Greek priestesses of Artemis in their temple (the town band shell) or astronauts landing on an alien planet (the big rock outcropping behind the Methodist church) or brave sailors battling pirates on the deep blue sea (the Anthonys' koi pond). If we strayed too far, Kitty would rein us in with a blast on her whistle, which Mom had given her to call me with back when I was only three.

That whistle ruled my childhood. It was made of bright blue plastic with a hard little ball inside that danced around when she made it shriek. It stopped me at the edge of danger and excitement, pulling me reluctantly back to Kitty. Even though part of me resisted, I always obeyed.

Once Kitty was too sick to take me, getting together with

Jess outside of school became difficult. My parents were too preoccupied to arrange for me to see Jess. I wasn't good at making plans once Kitty got sick, either, and afterward—I felt too cold and paralyzed.

Kitty's death set me apart at school. For a while the girls were extra nice to me in a distant way. April gave me her second cookie at lunch, and Keisha held the door for me as if I had a broken ankle. But whenever I tried to join a group that was laughing and talking, they would fall into a polite silence, and I would leave and go find a book to read.

Looking back at it now, I think if I could have jumped in and laughed with them, they might have forgotten to treat me differently.

I understood when Jess started spending more time with Keisha—hanging around with me wasn't much fun. Then Jess's dad got a new job and the Anthonys moved out of state.

Starting middle school was the hardest. My new school was a long bus ride away. Three elementary schools fed into it, so I didn't know most of the kids. That could have been an opportunity to reinvent myself as someone happy and normal, but I missed my chance.

The teachers called me by my whole name, Susannah, but April called me Sukie, and some of the boys misheard the pronunciation, probably on purpose.

"Is your name really Sucky?" asked Tyler Spinelli.

"No, it's Sukie," I said. "It rhymes with *cookie*. It's short for Susannah."

"Sucky Sukie!" said Cole Farley, Tyler's friend. They poked

each other, laughed, and started chanting it. "Sucky Sukie! Sucky Sukie! Sucky Sukie!"

I tried to ignore them. I managed pretty well. They were just boys, after all. It was harder when the girls started to whisper.

"Is it true Sucky's sister is dead?" Ava Frank asked Keisha on the bus. She kept her voice down, but I still heard her.

I couldn't hear Keisha's answer.

"You mean right in their house? A dead body? That's gross! Like in her *bedroom*?" said Ava, a little louder.

Keisha said something else I couldn't hear.

"I bet it's haunted," said Ava. "Sucky lives in a haunted house. That must be why she's so weird."

"Sh, Ava!" hissed Keisha audibly. "Don't be mean. She's sitting right there!"

Ava lowered her voice to a whisper and giggled. I didn't mind that so much. But I minded when Keisha giggled back.

That afternoon was the first time I blew Kitty's whistle.

Kitty gave me her whistle on her deathbed. When the doctors at the hospital said there was nothing left to do but keep her comfortable, Mom and Dad brought her home. They rented a hospital bed, the kind with a cold metal railing on the side and control buttons to raise the head or the foot.

Her first day back, Kitty called me into her room with a blast on her whistle. She was excited to be home, and she seemed better. Her cheeks were pink, like they used to be. "Come up here, Sukie!" she told me in her low, hoarse whisper, patting the spot next to her. "Check it out. It's a robot bed!"

The bed took up a lot of the room. Dad had had to push the dresser aside, and I remember noticing a strip of dust against the wall behind where it had been. But Kitty was home! Maybe now she would get well again. I crawled up next to her, and she pressed the button to raise the head. It made a low humming, grinding sound as it lifted us up and bent us forward from the waist. "That's so cool!" I said. "Can I try?"

"Wait, I want to show you the feet first." She pressed the button to elevate our feet, bending us up into a U. Then she lowered our heads so we were lying on a downward slope. She rocked us back and forth, our heads and feet waving slowly up and down like the tentacles of sea anemones.

"Come on, Kitty, let me try! It's my turn!" We wrestled for the controller, laughing.

That wasn't the last time I heard her laugh, but it was the last time it really seemed natural—the last time I forgot that it might be the last time I heard it.

I was alone with Kitty the day she died. The doctor had rung the doorbell, and Mom had gone downstairs to let her in. Dad was out on a construction job. He didn't want to take it with Kitty so sick, but we couldn't afford for him not to.

Kitty had her eyes closed. Her skin looked gray and her freckles stood out. "Where's Mom?" she whispered.

"Downstairs talking to the doctor. Want me to get her?"

She moved her head no. The movement was too weak to call it a shake. "Don't leave me alone. . . . I think it's happening. . . ."

"*What's* happening?"

"You know."

"It is not!" I said. "Who's going to take care of me if you're not here?"

She opened her eyes and crawled her hand across the blanket to reach mine. "I am. No matter what. Always. I promise." Her hand was icy cold, and her voice was so weak it was barely a whisper.

"But you can't, if you're dead!" I spit out the word like a curse. I knew I was making her feel bad, but I didn't care. I had to stop her.

She pointed to the little table next to the bed. I thought she was asking for water, so I picked up the glass. I'd gotten good at dribbling it carefully between her lips without going too fast for her to swallow and spilling it on her neck and pillow.

She moved her head no again. "The whistle," she whispered.

I picked it up and put it in her hand. She pushed it back into mine. "Use it. If you need me. I'll come," she breathed. "Okay?"

"No, Kitty," I said. "Don't go."

"I'm sorry, Sukie," she whispered. "But I'll come. I promise." Then she shut her eyes.

"Kitty?" I said. She lay still. I squeezed her hand, but I couldn't tell if she squeezed back. If she did, she did it too weakly for me to feel it.

"Mom!" I yelled. "Dr. Robbins!" They came running upstairs, but Kitty didn't open her eyes again.

I didn't blow the whistle at all that school year. At first, I was too mad at Kitty for dying. I didn't want to do anything she'd told me to do.

Later, I still didn't blow the whistle because I was afraid nothing would happen. Kitty would stay dead and leave me alone in this flat, bad world, and I would be mad at her all over again for breaking her promise.

But the day Ava called me weird and Keisha laughed, I went home and threw myself on Kitty's old bed and cried till my teeth tingled. Then I got up and went into my bedroom. I crawled under my bed and pulled out my secret box where I kept my treasures. It was an old cedar jewelry box of Grandma O'Dare's, lined with faded pink satin with a mirror in the lid. It smelled like Grandma O'Dare's face powder. I saw my tear-stained face in the dusty mirror as I dug through the contents: the silver dolphin pendant I'd found in the gutter behind Wax-man's Drugstore; the postcards Jess sent the summer she went to Switzerland with her family; my guppy, shark, and barra-cuda badges; the pencil I used to sign my name when I got my first library card. And Kitty's blue plastic whistle.

I held it in my hand. It rattled a little. It was smaller than I remembered, but its color hit a low, reverberating note of fa-miliarity like a tuning fork struck on the inside of my sternum.

I lifted it to my lips and blew.

The whistle screamed. It called me urgently with its well-known voice, tearing into *now* from the impossible past, the gone-forever. I felt as if something had been ripped open—maybe me, maybe the universe.

And then, through that rip, I felt a presence. Kitty.

I should have been scared, but I wasn't. Instead, I felt over-whelming relief that I'd been set free from the fake, flat, bad world where Kitty no longer existed and allowed to return home to the real world where she did.

I didn't see her, not that first time. We didn't speak. I just knew she was there. It wasn't until later that I started to understand how complicated it can be to have a ghost sister.

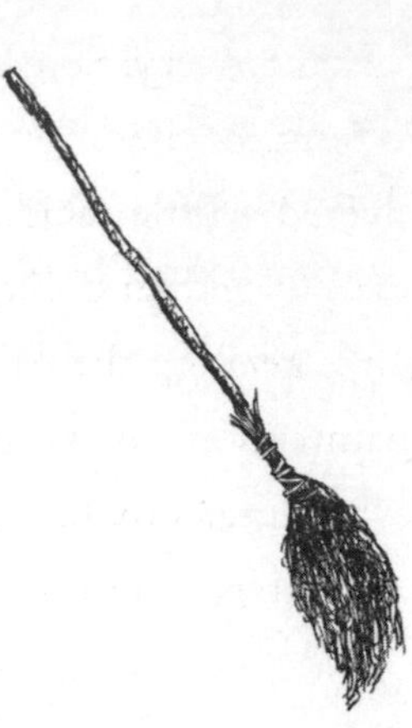

CHAPTER FOUR

A Broom and a Pipe

My parents and I finished packing the truck and drove down to the city early on Sunday morning, leaving well before dawn. Dad had rented a booth in the flea market in Hell's Kitchen, the one in the basement of a building that used to be a car showroom. Sometimes we go to one of the schoolyard markets in Manhattan or Brooklyn or the big outdoor parking-lot market in SoHo, but Dad thought the snow would keep the customers away this weekend.

Our allotted spot in the flea market was near the door. Scraps of paper and old leaves had blown in, so I got the old broom out of the truck and swept them up before we unloaded the furniture. We set up the long folding tables and unrolled an old tribal rug to make our space look more welcoming.

Mom and I unwrapped the smaller items and set them out. There's an art to arranging a flea market table. You want to space things out enough that people can see what you're selling and imagine the things in their own homes. But you also want enough interesting clutter that they can think they're making a brilliant discovery. Some people like things better when they have to hunt for them.

I covered a little table with a tablecloth and laid out a tea service for two, then stacked linens and china nearby. I lined up the lamps, keeping the pairs together. Mom leaned the paintings against the wall and put out a box of old frames. We put a big $10 clutter box on the end of each table and seeded the boxes with items from the good-stuff stash we kept under one of the tables, to be replenished throughout the day. The occasional treasure makes the junk look more tempting.

Dad went to say hi to the other sellers he was friends with and see if they had anything he wanted to buy for our customers. And the other sellers visited us, doing the rounds before the doors opened. Mom had saved some scarves for Rosetta, who specializes in twentieth-century vintage clothing; she bought six of them. Mr. Alton offered his opinion on a big, dingy landscape—1880s, not worth cleaning, might have more appeal in Brooklyn—and bought two of the small wooden frames.

The morning was pretty slow. A young woman bought a handful of silver-plate flatware from the 1930s. A man measured the big oak secretary desk and said he would bring his wife to check it out, but he never came back. Everybody asked Mom how much she wanted for the bronze deco box with the greyhound finial, but nobody bought it.

I'd forgotten to bring my homework, so I chose a book from a stack of 150-year-old novels and settled down to read. Just before lunchtime, Dad went off to meet a potential client who was planning to remodel the kitchen in her country house, leaving Mom and me to mind the booth.

A woman stopped to look at a lamp. "That's sweet. How old is it?" she asked Mom. Reaching for it, she knocked over a chipped pink vase. She lunged for it but missed, and it smashed on the cement floor. "Oh, I'm so sorry!" she said. "I'll pay for it, of course."

Mom smiled tensely. I could see her calculating the potential price of the vase against the goodwill she might earn by not making a fuss. Maybe if Mom was nice about the vase, the woman would feel bad enough to buy something else. "Don't worry about it," Mom said. "Accidents happen. Sukie, honey, can you reach the broom?"

I swept the broken vase into a newspaper, leaned the broom against a walnut bookcase, and took the fragments to the trash. When I came back, the woman was counting out money and Mom was wrapping up the lamp. Apparently her calculation had worked.

As I returned to our booth, I smelled something unpleasant—dense and smoky, like chocolate doused with sulfur—and found a man eyeing my broom. The smell was coming from his pipe, a fancy one with a painted bowl and an amber mouthpiece.

Some flea market shoppers like to dress pretty wildly. Usually they favor old-fashioned styles: long dresses, maybe, or bell-bottoms and love beads, as if they just stepped out of 1914 or 1967. But this man had on extravagantly fashionable clothing. His suit was clearly new, with a subtle gray stripe shot through with threads of dull purple. He carried an expensive-looking coat over his arm. His tie—a light, bright red that was almost pink—matched his hat. He had picked up the broom and now turned as if planning to walk off with it.

"Can I help you?" I asked.

Startled, he dropped the broom, then picked it up again. "How much is this?" he asked. His voice had a too-sweet, hissing quality, and he was spreading stinky pipe smoke all over our booth.

"It's not for sale," I said. "And I don't think you're allowed to smoke in here."

The man puffed on his pipe and waved the smoke away. "I'll give you fifteen dollars," he said.

"No," I said, annoyed. "It's not for sale."

"Forty?"

"No," I said again. "It's not even mine—it's my cousin's." I grabbed the broom by the handle, but he didn't let go.

"A hundred and fifty dollars, and that's my best offer."

"I said *no*." I pulled on the broom. He still didn't let go. Were we going to have a tug-of-war?

The man took a deep pull on his pipe, which flared up red, just the color of his tie and hat. Then it went out. His grip on the broom slackened, and he let go. I stumbled back, suddenly off balance, holding the broom.

The man turned his back and bent over his pipe, muttering something. Why had I thought he was so well dressed? Now his suit jacket looked faded and shabby.

Mom finished talking to the lamp woman and came over. "What's that smell?" she asked. "Is something burning? I'm sorry, sir, but there's no smoking here."

The man straightened up, his pipe lit again. No, I had been right the first time: His clothing was perfectly new and hideously elegant. He bowed slightly and left, still smoking.

Mom waved away the smoke with the real estate section of the newspaper. "Phew," she grunted. "What a smell! I hope it doesn't drive away the customers. What did he want?"

"The broom. He wanted to buy it."

"Really? How much did he offer?"

"Kind of a lot," I said. "But it's not ours—it's Cousin Hepzibah's."

"Hm," said Mom. "A lot? How much?"

"Mom! You promised! And he was really creepy."

"You're right, Sook. I won't sell it without asking Hepzibah. Even if it's just a broom. I wonder if it's Shaker. Those old Shaker brooms and brushes can bring a good price. We should check it out when we get home. Ready for a slice of pizza?"

"Sure, I can go get it. What do you want on yours?"

"No, you stay here. You know I don't like you wandering around the city by yourself. Will you be okay watching the booth alone? Maybe we should wait for Dad."

"I'll be fine, Mom. Pepperoni, please."

Mom frowned. "I'll tell Tom and Tim to keep an eye on you. Shout for them if there's any trouble, okay? Promise?"

"I promise," I said.

"Okay, back soon." She kissed my cheek quickly and bundled on her coat.

I read my book for a while. I'd chosen it partly for the cool cover—faded red cloth embossed with gold arabesques—and partly because I recognized the author's name, Laetitia Flint, from Cousin Hepzibah's library. It was a gothic story teeming with orphans, shipwrecks, tumbledown mansions, missing wills, and exclamation points. I was pretty sure the mysterious figure swathed in gray was going to turn out to be a ghost.

"Excuse me?"

I looked up. Then I looked farther up. A guy was standing by the table holding a small, dusty old bottle. He looked approximately my age, but twice as tall.

I closed my book on my finger and smiled up at him, telling myself not to be timid. People my age make me feel shyer than adults. I guess because of all the mean kids at school. Besides, he was quite good looking.

"How can I help you?" I asked.

"I'm looking for old bottles like this," he said. "Could be glass, could be stoneware. Preferably with the original contents. Got anything like that?"

"I don't think so, but you're welcome to look. If we did, they would be in there," I said, pointing to the clutter boxes.

Leaning down, the guy started rummaging through a box. Drops of water glinted in his hair and on his coat. Raindrops or melted snow? Snow, I hoped—Mom hadn't taken an umbrella. "Hey, what's the weather like up there?" I asked.

The guy straightened up and gave me an exasperated look. "Exactly the same as the weather down there, where you're at. The climate doesn't change a whole lot in a few feet. And please don't tell me I must be great at basketball. I'm not. I never was. I suck one hundred and ten percent, and the next person who gives me a hard time about it, I'm going to throw them through a hoop. Though," he added, "I'll probably miss."

"What?" I said. "Oh, no! That's not what I meant at all! I just meant is it snowing or raining outside? Upstairs, I mean. Because your jacket is wet."

He looked down at his shoulders and brushed at them with his hands. "Oh. Right. It's snowing. Sorry I snapped at you. Everybody's always going on about how tall I am and it gets real old."

"I can imagine," I said.

"You think you can, but you can't. Especially because my big brother—he was a basketball star, so everybody expects me to be too."

"And you really can't play?"

"Nope. Not basketball, not football, not nothing," said the tall guy. "Chess. I'm good at chess."

"Of course you are," I said. "Tall people are always good at chess."

That made him smile. "Yeah. 'Cause we get a better perspective on the board."

"If you're missing a knight or something, I think there are some vintage chess pieces in that box," I said. "Maybe a whole set."

"Thanks." He poked around in the box I'd pointed to, picked something up, and turned it over in his hand. Then suddenly he stood up straight again and yelled, "Libbet! Libbet!"

He waited, but nothing happened. He put two fingers in his mouth and let out a piercing whistle. "Libbet! Libbet!" he yelled again.

Nothing continued to happen. Nothing went on happening for a while. I wondered who he was calling.

He whistled again, and an enormous dog came galloping down the empty row between the sellers' stalls.

Some of the people at the flea market like to bring their dogs with them. Tom and Tim, who sell antiquarian books and maps and antique lab equipment, have a big yellow Labrador retriever named Pauli. He's sweet and sedate and likes to go to sleep with his nose on your shoe. The lady with all the waffle irons has a toy poodle. But I had never in my life seen a dog like this one. It was the size of a sheep—no, a lion. It seemed like an expensive dog to take to a flea market, I thought, remembering the broken vase. Wouldn't it knock stuff over?

The dog skidded to a stop in front of the guy. It leaned down its head and snuffled at the object he was holding. It gave one brief, quiet bark, then insinuated its large body between the tables and snuffled at my legs.

I held out my hand. The dog sniffed, decided I was okay, and gave my hand a gigantic lick. It didn't seem to be knocking anything over. "Hello, Libbet," I said, scratching behind its ears. They were the size of sweaters, but silkier.

The chess guy cracked up, as if I'd said something hilarious.

"What's so funny?" I asked.

"That's not Libbet," he said, choking with laughter. "That's Griffin."

"Oh," I said. How was I supposed to know that? "Hilarious."

"Sorry," he said, "it's just—well, you'll see. Griffin! Griffin, go find Libbet."

The dog politely removed its head from my hand and

bounded gracefully away. Soon it came back, leading a young woman. She had snowflakes in her light brown hair and was wiping snow off her glasses with a cloth handkerchief.

"That's Libbet," said the chess guy. "Griffin's a dog. Libbet's a person."

The woman put her glasses on and held out her hand. "Elizabeth Rew," she said. She had a nice smile. "Call me Elizabeth—Andre's the only one who calls me Libbet. He's right about one thing, though. I'm a person."

"Susannah O'Dare," I said, shaking her hand. "Call me Sukie. I'm a person too."

Griffin gave another brief bark.

"I know," said Elizabeth, "but you can't deny you're a dog."

Griffin tilted its head, and Elizabeth scratched it behind the ears. "Good boy," she said absently. She blew her nose with her handkerchief, then sniffed the air, frowning.

"Sorry about the smell," I said. "There was a weird guy here smoking a pipe."

"Hm," said Elizabeth.

"Libbet, the reason I called you, what do you think of this?" asked the guy—Andre—handing her the object in his hand. It was an old brass doorknob. It had a swirly pattern, like a new fern leaf before it uncurls.

Elizabeth closed her eyes and fingered the curves. Then she brought the doorknob to her nose and sniffed at it. She opened her eyes and nodded. "Well spotted, Andre," she said. She turned to me and asked, "Where is this from, do you know?"

"Some old house," I said. "In Vermont, I think."

"Do you know where exactly?"

"I'm not sure. The house is probably gone now anyway. My dad picks up a lot of stuff from demolitions."

"Would he remember where it was?"

"Maybe. I can ask him if you like. Or you can ask him yourself if you're going to be around for a while—he'll be back in an hour or so."

"Okay. We can come back," said Elizabeth.

"Don't we have to go meet Doc?" asked Andre.

"Oh, you're right." She turned to me. "Will you and your father be here again next weekend?"

"I'm not sure," I said. "It depends on the weather."

"We better get the doorknob, at least," said Andre.

Elizabeth nodded at him. "How much?" she asked me.

I tried to decide what my mom would charge. "Thirty dollars?" I hazarded. "It's brass."

Elizabeth took a ten and a twenty out of her wallet without argument. Darn, I thought. I should have asked for more.

I wondered about the relationship between the two of them. They didn't look like family, since he was African American and she was white. That didn't necessarily mean they weren't related, of course. Then there was the age difference: She couldn't be more than ten or fifteen years older than him. They seemed to know each other very well. She could be his teacher, maybe, but in that case wouldn't he call her Ms. Rew instead of some silly-sounding nickname?

Andre went back to poking through the boxes while Elizabeth looked over the things on the tables. Then she froze, the way people do when they spot something they really, really want, but they don't want you to know how much they want it. She casually picked up Cousin Hepzibah's broom, lifted it to her nose like the doorknob, and sniffed it.

"That's not for sale," I said quickly.

"Are you sure? I would give you a fair price. Maybe I could talk to your dad?"

I shook my head. "It's not ours—it's my cousin's," I said. "What is it with that broom? Is it Shaker or something? The guy with the pipe tried to buy it too."

"He did? What did he look like?"

"Short man, fancy clothes, red hat. Smoking a really stinky pipe. Kind of creepy somehow," I said.

Elizabeth and Andre exchanged glances. "You think it's Feathertop?" he said.

"Maybe," she answered.

"Who's Feathertop?" I asked.

"He's . . ." Elizabeth thought for a minute. "He's an agent for a private collector we know. You're right, kind of creepy. . . ."

"Why does he want the broom? Is it Shaker, like my mom thought?"

"No, I don't think so. The Shakers made flat, modern-style brooms. They invented them. This one has the traditional round shape. I think it's probably old, though—maybe very old."

"Like how old?"

She shrugged. "A hundred years? Two hundred? Old. If your cousin decides to sell it, will you or your dad call me first? And if someone else makes an offer, give me a chance to meet it? I would really appreciate it," she said. She took a business card out of an antique silver card case and handed it to me.

"Um, sure," I said, reading the card. It said *Elizabeth Rew,*

PhD, Associate Repositorian for Acquisitions, The New-York Circulating Material Repository. It gave a phone number and an address.

She handed me another of her cards. "Here's one for your dad too. Ask him to call me?" she asked. "I want to talk to him about that doorknob. Maybe he could keep an eye out for some other stuff for us too."

"Sure," I said again.

A man, maybe in his thirties, with salt-and-pepper hair and a suave look, appeared at her elbow. "Why, Elizabeth Rew! And little Andre too, looking smug. Can I assume you've beaten me to the good stuff again?"

Elizabeth turned around and smiled. "Hello, Jonathan. I was wondering if we'd see you—it seems we just missed your . . . associate."

Was this the creepy pipe smoker's boss, then?

"Yes, he told me there were treasures at this booth. Will you show me what you found?"

Elizabeth handed him the doorknob. "Very nice," he said, fingering it appreciatively. "Wharton, do you think?"

"Could be. It's too soon to tell," said Elizabeth.

"What'll you take for it?"

Elizabeth shook her head, laughing a little. "Pushy, pushy! Not for sale. You're too much, Jonathan! What about you—find anything good?"

He shook his head too. "Not today. I don't seem to have your luck. Unless there's something you missed here . . ."

Andre took out his cell phone and checked the time. "I don't think there is, but you can look. Come on, Libbet, we better go. Doc's waiting," he said.

“All right. Thank you, Sukie,” said Elizabeth. “Nice to meet you. Happy hunting, Jonathan. Come on, Griffin.”

The three of them disappeared up the exit ramp, the dog’s nails clicking on the cement.

The minute they were gone, Mr. Suave Salt-and-Pepper whipped around and picked up the broom. “How much for this?” he asked intensely. For the third time that day I had to insist it wasn’t for sale.

CHAPTER FIVE

Cole Farley

I rode the bus to school the next day—same school, different bus. I waited by the gate at the bottom of the hill, worrying that the driver would forget to stop for me. The bus showed up right on time, though.

My new stop came early in the route, so I got my pick of seats. I chose an empty row in the middle, hoping nobody would sit next to me, and opened my Laetitia Flint novel.

I was right about the mysterious figure swathed in gray: She did turn out to be a ghost. She drove the bad guys to their deaths one by one by materializing suddenly behind them and letting out eerie screeches as they walked along the cliff path above the churning maelstrom.

I thought it was pretty dumb of the bad guys to walk along the cliff path above the churning maelstrom. I didn't blame the first one or two bad guys, but after the third time it happened, the rest of them should have known better.

After a few stops, someone interrupted my reading. "*You're* not on this bus," said a boy's voice. I looked up and saw Cole Farley, horrible Tyler Spinelli's horrible friend.

"I'm not?" I said. "I must be a ghost, then."

"Maybe that's why they call you Spooky Sukie." He laughed—I wasn't sure whether it was at his own joke or mine—and slid in next to me on the seat.

I kicked myself. I should have kept my mouth shut.

"Seriously, what are you doing on this bus?" he asked.

Cole Farley was tall and handsome, with chiseled cheekbones, broad shoulders, clear skin, and straight, silky black hair. His good looks made him seem more hateful to me, not less.

"We moved," I said, turning back to my book.

"Really? Where?"

I wanted to tell him to mind his own business, but I remembered how mean he used to be, and I didn't want to provoke him. "Thorne Hill Road," I said.

"Where that weird old haunted house is, with the weird old lady? I didn't know there were any other houses up there."

"There aren't," I said.

"So where are you living, then?"

"I just told you. Thorne Hill Road. With my Cousin Hepzibah."

"The old lady in the haunted house is your *cousin*?" His silky black eyebrows shot up to the top of his high, hateful forehead. "Spooky Sukie is right!"

Oh, you foolish boy, I thought. I'm not the spooky one you should be worried about. My sister was probably listening to every word. These days, Kitty didn't always wait for my whistle before she showed up—I often felt her watching over me invisibly. Lately, she took her job as Sukie protector more and more seriously.

I glared at Cole and didn't answer.

"What's it like inside your cousin's house?" he went on, apparently completely unbothered by my glare.

"Old," I said.

"Yeah, but old *how*? It's so *big*! What are the rooms like? Is it just your cousin in there?"

"Hey, Farley! Cole!" Some of his friends at the back of the bus had spotted him. "What are you doing up there? Get back here and sit with us!"

"Okay, okay! Coming," he shouted. He gave me an apologetic half smile—did he think I would actually *mind* his leaving? "Catch you later, Spooky," he said and strode gracefully away to join his friends.

Cole left me alone on the bus home. So did everybody else. When I got off, I shouldered my backpack and started up the steep hill to the mansion that was now my home. Big black birds—crows, maybe—sat on the peak of each gable, cawing one by one as I approached.

"Sukie, is that you? Come in here a minute," called Dad from the carriage house. He had several cardboard boxes open on his workbench. "That doorknob you sold to the museum lady yesterday—remember what it looked like?"

"It was brass. Sort of ferny. Why?"

"She wants to know what house it came from and if I got anything else there. Come help me look."

"Okay. What am I looking for?" It was warm in the carriage house—Dad had a wood fire going in the potbellied stove. I shrugged off my backpack and coat.

"Another doorknob like the one she bought," he said. "Here, these boxes have stuff from different houses. Find the doorknob, you find the house."

I poked through the boxes of old hardware—doorknobs, hinges, knockers, mailbox slots, things like that. All the doorknobs in the first box were made of china, mostly plain dark brown, though a few had swirls in the glaze to make it look like wood grain. The ones in the next box were made of brass, but they were all oval, not round, and instead of the leafy design, they had intertwined initials on them. I wondered what it would be like to be so rich that you put your initials on your doorknobs. But maybe the letters stood for the name of a school or a hospital or something, not a person.

The third box had the doorknob I was looking for—I recognized its ferny swirls. I recognized something else too: The doorknob gave off an electrical coldness when I touched it. It was the same feeling I got when Kitty showed up in a room, the same feeling I got from the broom everybody wanted to buy. Was that what made Elizabeth want these?

Remembering how Elizabeth had smelled her doorknob, I lifted this one to my nose. It smelled like brass, just as you'd expect.

I didn't find anything else very interesting in that box. A couple of the hinges had a faint echo of the doorknob's electrical chill, and there was a bell attached to a neat spring mechanism, but that didn't feel alive like the doorknob. Well, *alive* wasn't quite the word—maybe *inhabited.* I twisted the bell, making it ring.

"Find anything?" asked Dad.

I held up the doorknob. "Here. Do you remember which house the stuff in this box came from?"

He nodded. "That was a great old one, with the beams and gingerbread trim, but in terrible condition. It was a shame they had to demolish it. Almost nothing was salvageable. All the floors were rotted through. And the bats in the attic!" He whistled. "The whole thing gave me a chill. Thanks, Sukie. Here, toss it back in." I dropped the doorknob in the box. Dad tore a piece of transparent packing tape with his teeth and sealed the box shut. He taped Elizabeth's card to the top. I wondered if she would want everything in the box, or just the doorknob and the chilly hinges.

Mom and Cousin Hepzibah were sitting at the kitchen table peeling potatoes. "Hi, sweetie. How was school?" asked Mom.

"Okay," I answered, as always. Even when things were bad, I never told Mom. But in fact, aside from Cole Farley's unexpected visit on the bus that morning, my day had been pretty uneventful. Nobody bothered me at lunch, and I'd gotten a 93 on last week's math quiz. It felt odd having such a normal day at school when everything at home was completely new and strange.

"Do you have everything you need in your room?" asked Cousin Hepzibah.

"Yes, thanks . . . or, actually, where's the vacuum cleaner? I want to try to get some of the dust out of the curtains."

"Ours is still packed," said Mom. "Hepzibah, do you have one?"

Cousin Hepzibah shook her head. "Not for years. It was

hard getting it up and down the stairs, so I didn't replace it when it broke."

"I'll unpack ours first thing tomorrow, then," said Mom.

"Oh, that reminds me. . . ." I spotted the broom in the corner behind the door and brought it over to Cousin Hepzibah. "What's the story with this?" I asked her. "Everybody kept wanting to buy it."

Cousin Hepzibah put down her potato and her knife and held out her hand. "Oh, my. This takes me back," she said with a faraway smile. "Where did you find it?"

"In the attic. I was using it to sweep out the truck, and then at the flea market, people kept wanting to buy it. You wouldn't sell it, would you?"

"Sell it? No, no. Not that broom. But of course it's up to you. It's yours now."

"Mine?"

"Oh, yes. I'm far too old to be running around with a thing like that." She smiled and put the broom back in my hand, closing my hand around the broomstick and patting it. "It's time for you to have it."

"I . . . Thank you, Cousin Hepzibah."

"Most of the things here will be yours, sooner or later," said Hepzibah.

"Much, much later, I hope," said Mom.

"I rather hope so too." Cousin Hepzibah picked up her potato and started paring again, the peel falling away in one long, narrow, curving ribbon.

• • •

That night, the ghost in my room was Kitty. She threw herself on my bed, sending up puffs of dust from the curtains. I know ghosts aren't supposed to have bodies, and Kitty didn't exactly—if you tried to hug her, your arms went right through her. But she could move things. She was particularly good with cold drafts and liquids; for weeks after that conversation about me living in a haunted house, Keisha kept shivering in the hallways and Ava Frank's milk spilled all over her lunch, over and over. Kitty did worse things too, sometimes; I was pretty sure when Ava's friend Ellie tripped and sprained her ankle after dropping my backpack in a slush puddle, it wasn't an accident.

One thing Kitty didn't do, though, was talk. That was okay. I knew her well enough to understand her anyway.

I was right: She had been listening to what Cole Farley said on the bus, and she didn't like it one little bit. I could feel the anger coming off her in waves. It was like standing too close to a barbecue on a windy day.

"I know he's a jerk, Kitty, but please leave him alone," I begged. "He's already calling me spooky. If you mess with him, it'll make things worse."

I could tell Kitty wouldn't mind teaching Cole a lesson, or his friends, either, but she reluctantly agreed not to bother them—for now. There were other things worrying her. She didn't think Mom should have left me alone at the flea market, and she didn't think I should talk to strangers there, especially not weird, creepy strangers. She thought I should probably just stay home. She wished I *could* stay home, but home was gone.

She hated leaving our old house. It wasn't the same here—she hadn't spent much time in this place before, it wasn't *hers*, and it made her feel weaker and somehow scattered. She liked Cousin Hepzibah, though.

I asked her about the other ghost, but she didn't seem to understand me.

"But you're a ghost yourself, Kitty!"

She gave me her patient impatient look, the one that says "My baby sister is talking like a silly little baby." With a sigh that fluttered the bed curtains, she floated off the bed and sank slowly into the painting over the fireplace. I got up and went over to it to look for her, but I couldn't make out much, just glimpses of a river through shadowy trees.

I wondered where Kitty went when she wasn't here. Was she in the picture now, behind a tree or over a hill, out of sight? Was she in the walls? Was she nowhere at all?

I felt as lonely as I had when she'd first died.

CHAPTER SIX

Supernatural Salvage

"Put on your boots, Sukie-Sue," said Dad a few days later. I was sitting in the kitchen with Cousin Hepzibah, the only really warm room in the house. I had finished my history homework and was reading ahead to see what would happen to George Washington's battered army, but I clapped the book shut and jumped up from the hearth bench. "Where are we going?" I asked.

"Possible salvage."

"Where?"

"New Hampshire."

Dad liked me to keep him company, especially after Kitty died. He didn't usually say much, but it was companionable driving with him.

After a while, we turned off the main road onto a gravel road that led uphill. A plow had been through after the last heavy snowfall, but that was days ago. Since then, a few light dustings had left the road ghostly between looming trees.

The view opened up dramatically when we got to the top of the hill. What must once have been a lawn sloped down from a large old house. Despite a tangle of scrub and leafless saplings, you could see clear across a town-spattered valley.

The house itself was tall and graceful, with a pillared porch that sagged in the middle. A young tree was growing next to the chimney, rooted in the roof. "They're tearing this down?" I asked.

Dad nodded.

"Why?"

He shrugged. "Cost a lot to fix it, and they like modern."

We went in, noting the heavy door and the windows on either side, each with sixteen panes of wavy glass. There was a built-in hall tree for hanging hats and umbrellas. It was in pretty good shape, its mirror glimmering dimly. The hall was surprisingly grand, with paneling and a marble mantelpiece.

The staircase listed scarily. "Mahogany," Dad said approvingly, knocking on the banister. The newel was carved into a pineapple.

"When's the house coming down?" I asked.

"Soon. Bruce says they want to start building in the spring."

That was good news. Dad's friend Bruce liked to hire Dad, and he always gave him first crack at the salvage. "And the property owners don't want to reuse any of this? Not even that awesome fireplace?"

Dad shook his head. "They're steel-and-glass people."

"What a waste." I patted the doomed pineapple finial.

When I touched it, something cold buzzed through my arm. It felt like the doorknob Elizabeth Rew at the flea market had bought, or the broom, or like the air just before Kitty shows up. I remembered how Elizabeth had sniffed at the doorknob.

Was she somehow sensing the same quality by smelling it that I sensed by touching it?

"You know what, Dad?" I said. "I bet that lady from the flea market last week is going to want this stuff."

"Really? Why?"

I shrugged. "I don't know, I just . . . get a feeling. Remember how she was so interested in where those doorknobs came from? I bet she'll want to see this place before it gets demolished."

He reached in his pocket and tossed me his cell phone. "Okay, call her. It's the last 2-1-2 number in my recent calls."

I couldn't get a signal indoors or out on the porch, so I climbed to the top of the hill behind the house.

"Elizabeth Rew, acquisitions," said the faraway voice in my ear.

"Hi, this is Sukie O'Dare. From the flea market—you bought a doorknob last week?"

"Oh, Sukie, of course I remember you. That was a great doorknob! Did you find anything more from that house?"

"Yes, another doorknob and some hinges. Dad's bringing them next weekend. But that's not why I'm calling."

"Oh? What's up?"

"We're in a house right now that Dad's friend is planning to knock down. We came looking for salvage. I thought you would want to see it before it's gone."

"That's so thoughtful. Tell me about the house—what made you think of me?"

"Well, it has some awesome details—paneling and mantelpieces and a really nice banister with a carved newel post, and

I don't know what else upstairs. But mostly it was just . . . I don't know, a feeling. The whole house somehow reminds me of that doorknob you bought."

"Say no more. You've convinced me. Where is this house?"

"Southeast New Hampshire, near the Massachusetts border. It's on a private road. I'm not sure about the name, but I think that's Granton Village down there. Hang on. I'll get the address from Dad."

"Does your phone have GPS? I don't need the address, if you could just text me the coordinates."

"Sure—hang on."

"Okay, got it," Elizabeth said when I got back on the line. "We're on our way. Thanks, Sukie, I really appreciate this. See you in a little bit."

"What—you're coming *now*? But it's hours from New York!"

"That won't be a problem. We'll be there very soon. Wait for us, okay?" She hung up.

"Okay," I said doubtfully, going back into the house. Maybe she was already in New Hampshire for some reason?

Dad was walking around upstairs, making the ceiling creak. "Watch out for that fifth stair," he called down to me.

I skipped the fifth stair altogether. The seventh wasn't in such great shape, either, but it held. I found Dad in a little room at the back, with a slanted ceiling and a broken window. A remnant of lace curtain flapped at the broken pane as if it was trying to get out, and the sill had rotted. On the mantel, someone had stuck a little bouquet in a jam jar a very long time ago. That cold feeling was strong in this room.

I handed Dad back his phone. "She wants to come look.

She says she'll be here soon. I guess she's in the neighborhood," I said.

"Huh," Dad grunted. "Hold that?" He gestured at the end of his tape measure. I helped him measure the wide pine floorboards, most of which were in pretty decent shape. He jotted the numbers in his notebook with a pencil and took pictures with his phone.

We'd gotten through the floors in three rooms when I heard a voice downstairs. "Hello? Sukie?"

I went out to the staircase and peered down. I saw three figures silhouetted against the door: Elizabeth, her enormous dog, and somebody very tall—that guy Andre.

"Wow, that was fast! We're up here," I said. "Watch out for the fifth stair."

"Mind if Griffin comes in? He's very careful," said Elizabeth.

"That's fine," I said, holding out my hand for the dog to sniff. He licked it and wagged his rear end—he had no tail. "It's not like he could ruin anything any more than it's already ruined. Just keep an eye on him—the floor's not in great shape and he's pretty big. It would be bad if he fell through."

Andre laughed. "Don't worry, Griffin always lands on his feet. Don't you, boy?" He and the dog took the stairs two at a time, stepping over both problematic stairs. Andre was wearing a pair of flip-flops with woolly hiking socks and dangling a pair of hiking boots by the laces.

Elizabeth followed more slowly. She had her boots on her feet and was carrying an old-fashioned walking stick. It looked like Cousin Hepzibah's cane.

Dad came out of the front bedroom and introduced himself.

"It's nice to meet you in person, Mr. O'Dare," said Elizabeth. "I brought Andre Merritt—he's a page at our library."

"Call me Kevin," said Dad, shaking hands with both of them. Andre shifted the boots to his left hand to free up his right.

"You didn't have to take those off," I said. "The floors are pretty far gone. A little snow won't make a difference."

Andre shrugged. "Habit, I guess," he said.

"How'd you get here so soon?" Dad asked. "Were you nearby?"

"Close enough," said Andre.

"This is a great area for hiking," said Elizabeth. "Cool house! You were right, Sukie. Mind if we take a look around?"

"Be my guest," said Dad. "Watch out—some of the floorboards are loose."

"It's okay, we're used to that," Elizabeth assured him.

Dad went back to taking pictures of the paneling in the front room. Andre walked over to the top of the staircase, squatted, and stared down the banister as if judging its straightness. He gave it a knock.

"It's mahogany," I said helpfully.

"Uh-huh. What do you think of this, Libbet?"

She leaned over the banister and sniffed. What *was* her sniffing all about? Could she tell mahogany by the smell? Or was she sniffing for something else? "It's the real thing," she said. Griffin sniffed at it too, then licked his nose.

I leaned over the banister myself and breathed deep, but all I could smell was dust and the moldy damp of a house with windows broken for decades.

Andre straightened his long legs and strode down the hallway, pausing every few steps to stare at a spot on the wall or the ceiling. There was something powerful and yet a little goofy about the way he moved, like a panther walking on its hind legs. Elizabeth followed him, sniffing. He opened the door to one of the bedrooms, and Elizabeth walked through.

"Hawthorne, do you think?" Andre asked. He had to duck so he wouldn't hit his head on the lintel.

"I'm pretty sure that's oak," I said, following them into the room.

He gave me a blank look. "What?"

"The door. I think it's oak, not hawthorn," I said. "The door frame, too."

"Oh. Yeah. It does look like oak."

"It's too late for Hawthorne," said Elizabeth.

"Irving?" suggested Andre.

What were they talking about?

"Irving's even earlier. And his stuff's all in New York," said Elizabeth.

"You're right," said Andre. "What about James or Wharton?"

"I guess it's possible, but most of those are European, and they're usually fancier," said Elizabeth.

"Not always. There's the Frome house," objected Andre.

"Mm. But that's probably in Massachusetts, and it's not really . . . you know."

"I don't know. It's gothic enough," said Andre. "But okay, I hear you."

"I'm thinking maybe Freeman," said Elizabeth, fingering a rag of curtain in the next bedroom. "No, maybe it's late Flint."

"Could be," said Andre.

"What *are* you guys talking about?" I asked.

They glanced at each other. "We're trying to figure out the origins of this house," said Elizabeth.

"You mean like who built it? Who the architect was?"

"Yes, something like that," said Elizabeth.

"It looks to me like it's from around the 1860s, 1870s," I said. "Maybe the owner would know. Dad can ask his friend."

"Thanks, Sukie. That could be helpful."

When they got to the bedroom in the back, the one with the glass of dead flowers, all three of them froze. Griffin gave a low, thoughtful growl. "Oh," breathed Elizabeth.

"Yeah," said Andre. "This is the real deal."

They went quickly down the landing to the front bedroom where Dad was kneeling by the fireplace peering up the flue. Andre had to duck again to get through the door. "We'll take it," said Elizabeth.

"Great," said Dad, getting up and brushing soot off his knees. "What do you want? Hardware, mantelpieces, bathtub? What about the appliances? There's a nice old range in the kitchen."

"All of it. The whole house," said Elizabeth.

"Oh." Dad sounded dubious. "I guess I wasn't clear. The property's not for sale, just the salvage. The new owner's taking down the house and putting up a new one on this site."

"No, I get that," said Elizabeth. "The repository I work for wants the building, not the land. We're making a collection of historic structures with certain . . . characteristics, and this house fits our collecting mission perfectly. We can take it off the owner's hands and save them the cost of demolition waste disposal. We'll use our own transport team."

"Oh." Dad didn't look so happy. "Well, Bruce generally lets me handle the salvage, and I usually help with the demolition. I guess this would be a cheaper option for him, but . . ."

Elizabeth said quickly, "Don't worry, you won't lose money on the deal. We'll be happy to pay your standard rates for whatever you would normally be salvaging, along with a finder's fee."

Dad brightened up. "I think we can work something out."

As Dad and Elizabeth discussed business details, Andre wandered out of the room, leaning down to inspect the chair railing that ran along all the walls.

I followed him, trailing my fingertips along the railing. It felt cold and zingy, like the banister. "Hey, Andre, what's a page?" I asked.

He straightened up and looked down at me. "What?"

"Elizabeth said you were a page," I said. "What's that?"

"Oh. It means I work at the library," said Andre. "The repository. I re-shelve things and bring patrons the items they're borrowing, stuff like that."

"So is Elizabeth your boss?"

"Sort of. Not really. The head of the repository is both of our boss. But I mostly work with Libbet. I've known her since I was three. She's an old friend of my big brother."

"Ah." That explained their puzzling relationship, how they

seemed sort of related, but not quite. It was hard to imagine him three years old, though. Surely he was way too tall to ever have been that little.

Something else was confusing me, too. "Why is a library buying this building?" I asked. They couldn't be planning to use it for housing books. The layout was all wrong for that, not to mention how the place was falling down. "The books would grow mold in ten seconds flat."

He looked puzzled for a second. Then his frown cleared up. "No, this house won't *hold* a collection—it'll be part of one. The New-York Circulating Material Repository isn't a normal library. It has objects, not books."

"How can it be a library if it doesn't have books?"

"Well, technically it's a repository, not a library. It's a circulating collection of objects. Patrons can borrow all kinds of stuff, like doorknobs and teacups and bass guitars and wood lathes and—pretty much whatever you can think of."

"People borrow *doorknobs*?"

"People borrow all kinds of crazy things."

"But I still don't get why you want a whole falling-down house."

"We don't want just *one*. We want a lot of them. It's for our annex. We're building a collection."

"A *collection* of *houses*?"

"Mm-hm."

"Where would a library keep a collection of *houses*?"

"In a special annex facility."

That must be one big facility. "But why do you want *this* house?"

He raised an eyebrow and quirked up the left side of his mouth. "I don't know—*you* tell *me*! You're the one that found it."

I didn't have anything to say to that.

Dad and Elizabeth came out of the front room together, with Griffin looming behind them. The dog was so big that when he stood next to Andre he made Andre look average-height.

"I'll get our legal team working on the papers," Elizabeth said.

"Great," said Dad. "I'll talk to Bruce."

We all trooped downstairs, avoiding the fifth step.

"Can we drop you off somewhere?" asked Dad.

"No, thanks. We have transport. I'd like to stay a little longer, if you don't mind—take a look around down here," said Elizabeth.

"Sure," said Dad dubiously. There was no car or truck or anything in sight, just the two of them with the dog and their walking stick and hiking boots. Still, what were they going to do, steal the place? It's not like we didn't know where to find them. "Stay as long as you like," said Dad. "Just prop that log against the door when you leave, okay? The latch doesn't catch, and I don't want it blowing open."

"Will do." They waved from the porch as our truck crunched down the gravel road into the shadow of the trees.

CHAPTER SEVEN

A Ghost's Request

We started a new unit in science class the next day: physiology. Before the class ended, Ms. Picciotto told us the first lab assignment would be dissecting sheep hearts.

Whoops from the bloodthirsty and protests from the animal lovers.

"Yes, it's required," said Ms. Picciotto. "No, you can't dissect a vegetable instead. Okay, partner time. I want you in eight groups of two or three students each."

"How many twos and how many threes, Ms. Pitch?" asked Tabitha Day.

"That's a good question." Ms. Picciotto walked to the corner of the whiteboard where she put the extra-credit assignments. "There are twenty-one students in the class. How many ways can the class be divided into eight groups of twos and threes? And for even extra-er credit, how many ways would there be if I said you could work in groups of four, too?"

"*Can* we work in groups of four?" asked Deshaun Franklin. He and his three best friends liked to stick together.

"No," said Ms. Picciotto. "Just twos and threes. Go!" She clapped her hands.

The class started scurrying around like a video of atoms forming molecules in a chemical reaction. Naturally, nobody headed my way. I looked around for Tabitha—she wasn't exactly my friend, but she wasn't unfriendly, either. Maybe she would let me join her group. But she already had two other kids with her.

The scurrying stopped. Nine groups had formed: Four groups of three, four of two, and one of just me.

"Pretty close, but we have one person left over," said Ms. Picciotto. "Who has room for a third?"

"That's okay, Ms. Pitch," I said. "I don't mind working alone."

"Good science is collaborative," she said. "And there aren't enough hearts." She scanned the nearby groups, looking for somewhere to put me. "Becky and Jen?"

She could hardly have chosen worse. Becky Crandon aspired to a high place in the court of Hannah Lee, the reigning queen of middle school; the last thing she wanted was to be associated with someone like me. She looked as if she'd been told to wipe up her little sister's vomit with her favorite sweater.

"We can work with Sukie, me and Lola," said a guy's voice behind me. I turned to look. It was Cole Farley, standing with Dolores Pereira.

Becky flashed Cole a brilliant white smile. "Thanks, Cole! I owe you one," she said.

He smiled back, showing just as much dazzling teeth. "Not

a problem," he said. Becky looked as if Prince Charming had just given her the perfect shoe fitting.

"Okay, people," said Ms. Picciotto. "Don't forget your lab notebooks. You'll be picking up your hearts at the beginning of the next lab period, so be prompt."

Cole turned his toothy smile on me. "Hey, Spooky, ready to cut up a heart?" he asked.

I smiled wanly back. "Too bad it's just a sheep's."

Dad was out when I got home, and I didn't see Mom or Cousin Hepzibah. I heard water running in the ground-floor bathroom, though. Mom must have been helping Cousin Hepzibah take a shower.

I went upstairs to my tower room, half expecting Kitty to show up and make a fuss about Cole again. In the time since she'd died, Kitty had taken a dimmer and dimmer view of the kids around me. She expected them to be mean, which made sense—they often were. But she didn't realize she was often the reason. They couldn't see her, but the sensitive ones felt uncomfortable around her, which meant they felt uncomfortable around *me*, so they kept their distance. The milk spilling and so on kept the less sensitive ones away too. But Cole didn't seem to mind her. I hoped she wouldn't take stronger steps to chase him away. Not that I wanted him around, exactly, but I really didn't want Kitty making a fuss.

I dropped my book bag on the floor next to the little desk, which held a lamp, a blotter, a windup clock, and an old-fashioned telephone—the kind with a dial. I'd seen a lot of telephones like that at estate sales and flea markets, but I'd never actually used one. I lifted the receiver, but it seemed to be dead, and nothing happened when I dialed.

Shrugging, I bent to take out my homework. My scalp prickled, and I felt a cold draft on the back of my neck. Kitty, here to administer her scolding.

But when I turned to look, it wasn't Kitty. It was the ghost that looked like me.

In the daylight she appeared both clearer and less vivid than she had at night. I could see that she was older than me, maybe eighteen or twenty. She was standing in front of the east-facing window so that the light from the west fell full on her face—at least, it would have if her face had been solid. Instead, it streamed through her, making her glow like a girl made of light. Her sunlight-colored dress flowed to the floor from a narrow waist. Her hair, also the color of sunlight, flowed over full sleeves and bare, sunlight-colored shoulders.

The only thing about her that wasn't the color of sunlight was the box in her hands: a chest about the size of a turkey-roasting pan. It was made of dark wood bound with strips of iron and studded with iron nails. Or rather, maybe it had once been made of wood and iron. Like the ghost herself, it was insubstantial now, the ghost of a chest. It looked heavy, though—she held it as if it made her arms ache. I could see through it, but I couldn't see inside it. A smell of spicy roses filled the room.

"Who are you?" I asked. "What do you want?"

She let out a sigh almost too soft to hear and lifted the casket. "Find my treasure," she whispered.

"What is it? Where is it? Who *are* you?"

"Find my treasure," she whispered again.

Then the room seemed to darken, as if someone or something else had entered, something hard and oppressive. The ghost looked around, as if in alarm. The shapes and edges that defined her dissolved, and the second, oppressive presence vanished, too, washed away as she melted into sunlight, chest and all. It's funny. Kitty never spoke, but I always understood her. This ghost spoke clearly enough, but I had no idea what she wanted. What treasure? Did she mean the box?

It did look like a movie version of a pirate's treasure chest. I imagined the lid rising to reveal a yellow glow of gold. Pieces of eight, ducats, rings, jeweled brooches, tangles of chains. They would be heavy and cold. They would chink and clatter when I ran my fingers through them.

Was there a golden treasure hidden somewhere—buried, maybe? How would I find it? Could I keep it if I did? Could we buy our house back?

Kitty would like that.

"Where is it—where's your treasure?" I asked the air, but the ghost didn't come back.

I abandoned my homework and went downstairs. I found Cousin Hepzibah in the drawing room, sitting in her straight chair by the window, her cheeks still pink from the shower. A little table by her elbow held a cup of tea and her needlework. She was reading a book, but she looked up when I came in. "What's the matter, child?" she asked.

"Nothing, it's . . ." I hesitated, then went for it. "Cousin Hepzibah, who is the ghost?"

She took it calmly. "Which ghost?"

I looked around for somewhere to sit. At the other end of the room, two sofas and a couple of armchairs clustered together like a clique of kids from drama club, but the only chair at this end was the one Cousin Hepzibah was already sitting in. She wasn't using her little footstool, though, so I sat on that. "The woman who shows up in my room wearing the old-fashioned dress," I said.

"Young or old?"

"Young. She looks like me. She's carrying a box, like a small trunk."

"Ah. I expect that's your great-great-great-great— No, wait." She paused to count on her fingers. "Your great-great-great-great-great-great-great-great-great-aunt Hepzibah Toogood. Windy, they called her. It's been quite a while since I've seen her. How is she looking?"

"Transparent."

Cousin Hepzibah smiled halfway. "Yes, well, that does happen. Otherwise?"

"I don't know. Sad, I guess."

"Did she give you a message?"

I nodded. "She said to find her treasure."

Cousin Hepzibah looked sad too then. "Poor Aunt Windy. She's been searching for a long time. I never could find it myself, and now, well . . . too late for me." She shut her book and swept it in a semicircle, indicating her legs and the cane beside her chair. "You're young. Maybe you can help her."

"I can try. What *is* her treasure?"

"Nobody knows—at least, nobody *I* ever asked knew. Her story is unfinished, you know."

"Unfinished?"

She nodded.

"Is that why she's a ghost?"

Cousin Hepzibah nodded again doubtfully. "It could be. It's a long, sad story. She lost her husband. He was a sailor, and he got shipwrecked and took up with pirates. She lost her baby, too. She lost everything."

"Pirates!" I said. "Is it pirate treasure, then?"

"It could be."

"But where is it? Is it in the house? On the grounds?"

She shrugged. "Nobody knows that, either."

"I could ask Dad to keep an eye out when he's doing repairs," I said. "That would be a start, anyway."

Cousin Hepzibah pursed her lips. "Do you think that's wise? Your parents may be too young to understand."

"Too young!" They were in their *forties*! "But I'm even younger!"

"Ah, but you're young enough."

That made no sense.

Still, when I thought about it, I saw she was right. Young or old, I had always known my parents wouldn't understand about ghosts—that's why I'd never told them about Kitty. I imagined their hurt, angry, worried faces. No, I couldn't tell them about this.

The doorbell rang, a long melancholy chime, startling me. "Sukie, dear, would you mind?" said Cousin Hepzibah.

"Of course!" I jumped up and ran to the door.

I could feel Kitty skimming along beside me, radiating angry anxiety, as if she knew something bad was out there.

CHAPTER EIGHT

A Dead Phone Rings

A man in an expensive-looking coat with a leather briefcase was standing on the doorstep. He looked surprised to see me, then quickly hid his surprise in a fake-looking smile. "I'm here to see Miss Thorne," he said. "Hepzibah Thorne," he added—just in case I was Miss Thorne too, I guess.

"Is she expecting you?" I asked. I didn't know why, but I didn't like him. Neither, I could sense, did Kitty.

"Yes. I'm here on business." He said it politely enough, but I could hear undertones of "none of your business."

I wanted to shut the door in his face. This was Cousin Hepzibah's house, though, not mine, so I couldn't be rude. "This way," I said and led him down the creaking corridor to the drawing room.

"Miss Thorne, I'm Craig Jaffrey from Dimension Partners," said the man, crossing the room to Cousin Hepzibah's chair.

"Yes, I remember you perfectly well," she said drily. She indicated her cane and added, "You'll forgive me if I don't rise."

I noticed that she didn't ask him to sit down—not that there would have been anywhere for him to sit if she had. Well, he could have sat on the footstool. I forestalled him by plopping back down on it myself.

Mr. Jaffrey shifted his weight from one foot to the other and said, "Have you had a chance to think about our offer to buy the property here, Miss Thorne?"

Buy the property! My heart fell. Where would we go?

"Why, yes," Cousin Hepzibah said. "I had all the time I needed the day you first made your offer. My answer is still no."

My hands, I found, had been clenched so tight my fingernails were digging into my palms. I took a deep breath and unclenched them.

"Well, we certainly appreciate your consideration," Mr. Jaffrey said. "I was hoping I could explain the advantages a little better. I've brought some materials that I'm sure you'll find . . ." Here he looked around for somewhere to put down his briefcase. I saw him consider the little table at Cousin Hepzibah's elbow—the only table at this end of the room—but it was covered with Cousin Hepzibah's complicated-looking needlework.

He gave up, put his briefcase on the floor, squatted down, snapped it open, and took out a shiny folder with a too-bright photograph of some ugly buildings on the cover. He held it out to Cousin Hepzibah, who made no move to take it. After an awkward moment, he handed it to me instead.

"As you'll see when you take a look at that prospectus, Miss Thorne, we've upped our offer by a very considerable eleven and a half percent," he said, still crouching by his briefcase. The pose made him look like an overdressed frog. I could see his shiny scalp through his thinning hair.

"I don't think you're likely to receive a higher offer, and certainly not in the time frame we're looking at," he went on. "At your age, I imagine the expense and inconvenience of living in a house in this kind of shape would add to the appeal of making a move sooner rather than later. I really encourage you to take a look at those numbers. It's a very generous proposal. We would of course help you relocate to an appropriate facility, take care of your relocation expenses."

Cousin Hepzibah waited until he seemed to be done talking. Then she asked, "Mr. Jaffrey, do you know how old I am?"

"Why—no. I was taught it was never polite to ask a lady's age." He smiled an oily smile, rocking a little in his crouch. He looked very uncomfortable, and I wondered why he didn't stand up. Had he gotten stuck?

"I'm ninety-one years old," said Cousin Hepzibah.

Evidently he *had* gotten stuck. He leaned forward onto his hands and knees, put one leg forward, pushed down on the floorboards, and staggered to his feet.

"I have trouble believing *that*, Miss Thorne. You certainly don't look a day over—" He stopped, clearly unable to come up with a polite but plausible number of years that she didn't look a day over.

"I'm ninety-one years old," Cousin Hepzibah repeated. "My family has lived in this house for more than three centuries, and I have no intention of leaving it—certainly not in the little time I have left aboveground. So please don't waste any more effort."

"It's no effort at all, Miss Thorne. It's my pleasure."

Cousin Hepzibah continued, "Your best bet is to wait until

I'm dead and then try my heirs. But I warn you, we Thornes are a long-lived family." She glanced at me and added, "And I don't think you're making a very good impression on the younger generation. Sukie, child, will you show our visitor to the door?"

"I really appreciate your taking the time to see me this afternoon, Miss Thorne. I'll just leave you those materials to look over, and I'll come back in a week or two to see if you have any questions," said Mr. Jaffrey.

"No need," said Cousin Hepzibah.

"Oh, like I said, it's no trouble at all."

"Good-bye, Mr. Jaffrey," said Cousin Hepzibah. "Sukie?"

I got up from the footstool. Something in the room felt hard and threatening, as if the entire house and all the Thornes, living and dead, wanted the guy gone. For once, I thought, we all agree. "This way, Mr. Jaffrey," I said, heading down the corridor to the front door.

Mr. Jaffrey followed quickly. "You must be very concerned about your grandma, Suzy," he said.

"Both my grandmothers are dead," I said.

"What? No, I meant Miss Thorne. She's what, your aunt?"

"My cousin. Why would I be concerned about her?" I asked.

"Well, her age, for one thing. It must be very hard for her, living in this old wreck," he said. "All those stairs. Leaky roof. Freezing in here. Frankly, if she was *my* cousin or whatever, I would have found a clean, modern facility years ago where she could be well cared for. With the money my firm is offering, she could live out her last days in comfort with plenty left over for your college fund, hey? A nice new house, money for you and your brothers and sisters, I bet your dad would love a new car, something for a rainy day. . . . Talk to your parents about it. See if they can convince your cousin to do what's best for everyone."

He handed me his card. I was getting quite a collection of the things.

"If they ask me, I'll be sure to tell them what I think. Good-bye, Mr. Jaffrey."

Shutting the door behind him, I went back to the parlor. "What was that all about?" I asked Cousin Hepzibah.

She rolled her eyes. "Just the latest reptile. They've been at it for decades. Back in the middle of the twentieth century they used to want to build housing tracts and golf courses. Then it was shopping centers and office complexes. A 'spiritualist retreat' once—the old ones had a good laugh at that. I think this fellow is proposing a resort hotel. With a marina in the pebble cove. You can take a look at those papers of his if you're interested. As for myself, I intend to die here."

"No time soon, I hope! We just got here," I said, holding out my hand.

She took it and squeezed it. "No, no. Not for a little while yet."

Before dinner, I was getting out my science notebook to read over the lab assignment when the phone on my desk rang.

The dead phone.

I stared at it.

It went on ringing.

I picked up the handset, which was tethered to the body of

the phone with a curly cord, and held it to my ear. "Hello?" I said.

"Hey, is that Sukie?" A guy's voice came echoey and hollow, as if he was standing at the other end of a long tunnel.

"Yes?"

"Man, you're hard to find! Don't you have a cell phone?"

"Who is this?" I asked. The voice sounded familiar, but I couldn't quite place it.

"Oh, sorry! It's Andre—Andre Merritt from the New-York Circulating Material Repository."

"Andre? But how . . . where did you get this number? I didn't even know the phone worked!"

"Yeah, believe me, it wasn't easy. You should get a cell phone. Listen, got a minute?"

"You mean now?" I glanced at the clock on the desk. It said quarter to five; I had about an hour before I'd need to go downstairs and help with dinner. "Sure," I said. "What's up?"

"Great! Me and Libbet wanted to know, can you zoom down here and take a look at those doorknobs?"

"Zoom down where? What doorknobs?"

"The ones we got at the flea market. We need— Wait, hang on a sec. Libbet wants to talk to you."

There was a clacking noise and then Elizabeth Rew came on the line. "Hi, Sukie, I'm glad we reached you. Your dad's phone is going straight to voice mail, and I couldn't imagine how we would find you, but then Andre had the bright idea of using the Murray phone. I'd forgotten we had it in our collection. So do you have a few minutes for a quick visit? We were trying to classify these doorknobs you sold us, but we can't figure out what they do, exactly. You seemed pretty sensitive, so I thought maybe you could help."

"What the doorknobs *do*? Don't they open doors? I mean, when they're attached to them?"

"Yes, of course, but beyond that. I thought if you could take a look, or get a feel for them, or whatever your sense is, you might be able to help pin it down. It shouldn't take long, if you can just pop over."

"Pop over where?"

"The repository."

"But isn't that down in New York? How would I get there?"

Elizabeth sighed. "This is kind of embarrassing, but I have zero sense of direction. I'm going to give you back to Andre, okay? He can give you directions."

A clatter again and then Andre came back on the line. "Okay, so, if I was you, I would just head east to the coast and then follow the coastline down. When you hit Connecticut, keep west of Long Island and head down along the Sound. It's dusk already, so you don't have to worry about attracting too much attention. When you hit Manhattan, zip down the east side and look out for Central Park—it's right near us." He gave an address, the same one on Elizabeth's card.

"But—but I can't drive! And it's hundreds of miles! And even if I could, Dad's got the truck."

"What truck? I thought you had a Hawthorne broom."

"A what?"

"Hang on." The phone clacked again, and I heard muffled voices, as if Andre were holding his hand over the mouthpiece. Soon he came back. "Hi, Sukie, sorry about the mix-up. Never mind now, but maybe we could borrow you next time you come to the flea market?"

"Um, sure," I said.

"All right, well, sorry, thanks again," he said. "See you Saturday, maybe."

"See you," I said.

The phone went dead. I stared at it for a minute, then hung up. What on earth was that all about?

CHAPTER NINE

A Bat and a Broomstick

That night, I was awoken again. I'm going to kill that ghost, whoever it is, I thought. So what if it's already dead?

But it wasn't a ghost this time. It was a bat.

In theory, I love bats, ever since I did a report on them in sixth grade. They eat mosquitoes. They pollinate banana trees. They're mammals just like us, but they have a whole extra sense—echolocation—and they can fly! Imagine being able to fly!

Loving bats in theory is one thing; loving the one that woke me up at 3:09 a.m. with its frantic twittering is another.

How did it get into the room, anyway, with the windows shut? Did it fly down the chimney? I jumped out of bed, pulling the bed curtains shut behind me, and hauled a window open with a shriek of rusty iron. The bat was flying around the room in irregular, darting circles, occasionally smashing into the wall.

"The window's that way," I said, pointing helpfully.

The bat flew into one of the closed windows instead. It

clicked and veered off toward the ceiling. At the very top of the wall it found a perch on the molding. It folded itself and hung shaking, like a tiny, miserable umbrella.

"Great. Are you just going to hang there all night?" I considered leaving the window open and getting back in bed, hoping it would find its own way out, but the room was freezing. "Come on, bat!" I reached up with the broom, hoping to persuade the bat to climb on so I could carry it to the open window. Even standing on the desk, though, I couldn't reach the bat.

I put the chair on the desk and climbed up. Almost! "Come on, little guy, get up," I said, leaning forward as far as I could and reaching out with the broom.

The chair tipped and fell over.

I yelled a curse. "Help! Help!" The chair crashed to the floor, but to my surprise, I didn't. The broom seemed to have caught on something. I held on as tightly as I could, looking around wildly to see what was holding it up. Not just *holding* it—pulling it. The broom was rising to the ceiling.

The bat, noticing an enormous person-and-broom combo heading its way, let go of the molding and started darting and flapping in circles again. The broom decided to follow it.

"No!" I screamed, hanging on for dear life, trailing behind the broom like a pair of overalls pinned to a laundry line in a hurricane.

The bat chose that moment to discover the open window and fly out of it. The broom headed for the window, flapping me behind it. "No, broom!" I screamed. "STOP!"

The broom stopped stock-still in midair. Inertia slammed my legs into the wall. "Ow!" I howled. I took a deep breath. "Go down now, please, broom. Slowly!"

Gently as a dandelion seed, the broom floated down to the floor and set me on the hearth rug.

My heart pounding, every muscle in my body trembling, I let go of the broom, collapsed on the floor, and rolled up into a little whimpering ball.

Mom heard me screaming and crashing from two floors away and came to see what was wrong. When I told her about the bat—I didn't tell her about the broom, of course—she insisted on checking me all over for bites and scratches, in case the bat had rabies.

"It didn't bite me! It didn't get anywhere near me," I protested. "And most bats don't have rabies, anyway. Only like one out of hundreds."

"That's one too many." Mom isn't as obsessed as Kitty with accidents and criminals, but diseases completely freak her out. She wanted to take me to the emergency room for rabies shots.

"Really, Mom, it didn't get near me."

"How do you know? You were asleep."

"I was shut up in bed with the curtains closed. Bats can't fly through curtains! When I heard it flapping around the room, I opened the window, and it flew out."

Mom frowned, wanting to believe me. We really couldn't afford an emergency room visit. "What was all that crashing and screaming, then?"

"Just me trying to get the window open. And shut again."

"Aren't bats supposed to spend the winter hibernating in bat caves? What was it doing here this time of year?"

I shrugged. "Spring's coming early? Or maybe it's a vampire," I said. "This place is spooky enough." My voice caught.

Mom hugged me. "Oh, honey," she said. "I miss our house too. Now that we're not trying to pay that mortgage, maybe I can go to nursing school. There are good jobs in health care. And work's sure to pick up more for Dad in the spring. These things are cyclical."

"Nursing? Wouldn't that make you too sad? Because of, you know . . ." I didn't want to say Kitty's name. She might hear me.

"I was thinking I could work with elders. Helping Cousin Hepzibah doesn't make me sad. But this is a daytime conversation, and you need your sleep. Why don't you come spend the rest of the night downstairs with me and Dad?"

"Oh, Mom! I'm not a baby. I'll be fine—the bat's not coming back. You should have seen how fast it went, once it found the window."

I lay awake for a long time after Mom left, wondering about the bat and thinking about the broom. Of course, I'd known about ghosts for a while. Were magic brooms really so different?

But somehow ghosts don't seem as—I don't know, as *weird* as flying broomsticks. I was so used to Kitty that she seemed like part of the natural world. Even though she could do things like making mean girls trip and fall and sprain their ankles. I thought of her as an extension of ordinary life. A dark extension, maybe, but still part of life.

Magic brooms, though—that seemed impossible, like something out of a fantasy book.

Apparently Kitty thought so too. She let me sleep, or try to, but when I stumbled blearily onto the bus the next morning, she took the seat next to me and expressed her disapproval. I should *not* be chasing bats around on flying broomsticks. For one thing, flying broomsticks were *way* more dangerous than *bicycles*, even. And I had no idea where that bat had been. Bats were like flying *rats*! It could be carrying all kinds of diseases! And I hadn't even washed my hands afterward!

I looked around. Evidently nobody else could see Kitty, so at least there was that. But I couldn't really talk back—nothing enhances a girl's reputation quite like having a fight with her invisible dead sister on the school bus.

I got out my book—another Laetitia Flint novel that I'd borrowed from Cousin Hepzibah—and tried my best to ignore Kitty, but it was hard to drown her out. I had to read each sentence three times.

The bus stopped to let some kids on, then lurched forward again. "Hey there, Spooky," said Cole Farley, dropping his book bag next to me.

"That seat's taken," I informed him.

"Yeah? By who, your imaginary friend?" He threw himself down with a flourish—right through Kitty.

I gasped. Kitty didn't vanish. She stayed there, sort of interspersed with Cole. She looked pissed.

Cole shivered. "Ooh, I feel an eerie chill! Is your imaginary friend a ghost?"

"I wouldn't joke about ghosts if I were you, Cole. You never know who—or what—might be listening. Now, is there something you want?"

"I want to take a nice, scenic bus ride with my lab partner," he said. "It's crowded in the back."

I started to tell him to go away, but instead I shrugged. It *had* been pretty nice of him to ask me to join his lab group. Even though he probably just did it to make Becky Crandon happy.

Kitty let me know what she thought of Cole in pungent terms—at least, they would have been pungent if she'd been using actual words. She tugged his T-shirt sideways, twisting it around his torso.

He squirmed uncomfortably. "Hey, what's your cell number? I need to be able to reach my lab partner."

"I don't have a cell phone."

"You're kidding, right? *Everybody* has a cell phone."

"Everybody except me."

"How come? Are your parents paranoid about Internet stalkers or something?" he asked. "Do they limit your screen time? Is that why you're always reading?"

Kitty pushed her face through his and hovered so it looked as though Cole was wearing a scowling Kitty mask. If I hadn't been worried I would seem like a complete lunatic, it would have made me laugh. "I don't have a cell phone because my family is poor, okay? We can't afford it."

"How can you be poor? You live in that gigantic mansion."

"We live in my *cousin's* gigantic mansion. Which is kind of falling apart. Otherwise we'd be homeless." I knew I shouldn't be saying these things—I could just be handing over ammunition for him and Tyler and those creeps to blast me with. But I told myself that not being able to afford a cell phone was nothing to be ashamed of—jeering at people for not being able to afford a cell phone was.

Cole took my outburst in stride. "Oh, okay. That makes sense. You know one of the things I really like about you, Spooky?" he said.

I gave him a "yeah, right" look. Yeah, right, there was even one thing he really liked about me.

"It's that you're so gloriously, magnificently weird."

Kitty took a lock of his hair and poked it into his left eyeball. He screwed his eyes shut and shook his head hard.

"Me? *I'm* weird? You're the one who's making crazy faces!"

He pushed his hair out of his face and went on, "Like, my other friends, I always know exactly what they're going to do next. Don't get me wrong—they're great guys—but they're so predictable. Right now Tyler and Ben are going to get into a big argument about who has a better defense, the Tigers or the Cardinals. Then Garvin is going to make a fart joke and Tyler is going to sit on him, and he's going to knock Ben's backpack over and everything's going to spill out, because Ben never remembers to zip it closed. Am I right or am I right?" He jerked his head toward the back of the bus, where his horrible friends were making a racket.

"Whereas you," he went on, "are sitting here reading a million-year-old book you stole out of a mummy's crypt. At least, that's what it smells like. And it's not even for school."

"That's why you think I'm weird? Because I like to read?"

"It's not so much *that* you like to read as *what* you like to read."

"Uh-huh. I'm going back to my book now. I'm at an exciting part," I said. "The heroine is telling the villain exactly what she thinks of him."

"Read away," he said. "I'll just sit here."

And he did, only squirming a bit, and cursing softly when Kitty pinched the cap off his pen, stabbed him with the point, and made ink leak all over his pants.

CHAPTER TEN

Learning to Fly

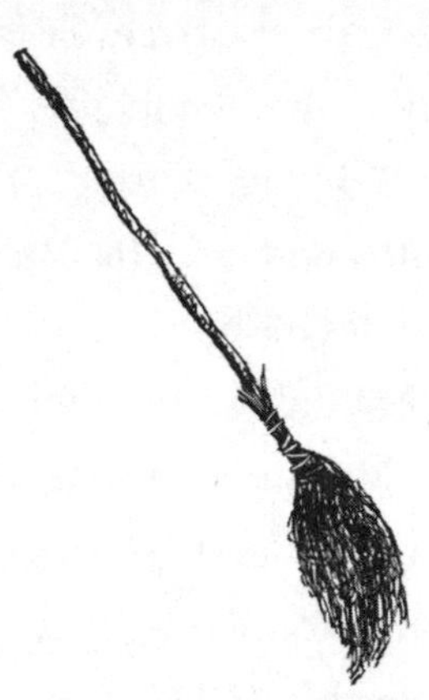

I needed to know more about this broomstick. Andre had called it a Hawthorne broom—maybe he had more information. But how could I reach him? I remembered I had Elizabeth's phone number. When I got home from school, I dug out her business card and tried dialing the number on my dead desk phone, but it didn't work.

If I couldn't reach Elizabeth and Andre on the phone, maybe I could just fly down to the city. I had the address. That must have been what Andre had meant when he told me on the phone to pop over. But what if they weren't there? I had no idea what hours they worked. And anyway, I'd better practice some more before I tried to cover hundreds of miles on a saddleless broomstick.

I took the broom out to the field behind the patch of woods by the barn and tried it. It's not so easy keeping your balance on the round dowel handle of a broom. It dug into me uncomfortably when I sat astride, but when I tried sitting sideways I kept slipping off backward or forward. I found myself doing a lot of dangling. No wonder bicycles have saddles.

Still: flying!

I flew so far up that I could see the ocean stretched out flat to the distant horizon.

Kitty didn't think I should go up so high. She didn't think I should be doing this at *all*, but I should at least keep down to about knee level, preferably with a pile of nice wet leaves underneath. No no NO! Was I crazy? Not above the trees! I better stop this, right *now*, or *else*!

"What are you going to do, Kitty, haunt me?"

Kitty didn't think that was funny.

"Come on, Kitty! Why should you be the only one who gets to fly?"

I'm sure Kitty thought it was a lot easier when I was little and she could just pick me up and carry me when I started to run off into danger.

Still, once I got the knack of balancing—it involved bending my knees back and looping my feet up behind me—she started to relax.

It took me a while to figure out how to guide the broom. Telling it out loud where to go turned out to be unnecessary. The broom was sort of between a horse and a bicycle, or maybe a mule and a toboggan; if you shifted your weight to match your intentions, you could usually get it to take the hint.

Kitty thought I was getting pretty good, but could I do *this*? She showed me a loop de loop.

I could, as it happened, although I had a little trouble

hauling myself up on top of the broom again after I slipped down under it.

After some practice, I could also do a vertical ascent, a five-point turn at least as good as Kitty's, and a pretty good backward spiral, even though it's hard to see where you're going when you're flying backward.

On my second circuit, a branch grabbed my hat. Kitty cracked up. Then we had another game of tag, a game of keep-away with the hat—try keeping a ghost away from a hat when she can control the wind—and more loop de loops, until I managed one without slipping under the broom. After that, we both flopped onto the ground and lay panting (me) and laughing (both of us) while the damp soaked through my jeans.

I hadn't had so much fun with my sister since before she died.

"See, Kitty? I didn't get hurt, not even a little bit."

That, she let me know, was because she was here taking care of me.

After dinner, I filled half the divided sink with hot sudsy water and dumped the silverware and glasses in it. Yet another thing I missed from our old house: the dishwasher. Cousin Hepzibah pulled her chair over to the sink, picked up a dish towel, and dried the glasses as I finished rinsing them.

"Hey, Cousin Hepzibah," I said, "that broom you gave me. Is there anything else you can tell me about it?"

Cousin Hepzibah nodded. "Best to wear trousers," she said.

"Trousers?" I asked.

"Yes, long skirts tend to tangle and short skirts—well,

they're not very modest." So she did know about the broom's powers! No wonder she didn't want to sell it.

"And it's best to stay beneath the tree line during the daytime. You're more visible than you think."

"Did you use the broom a lot when you were younger?" I asked.

"Quite a bit, at one time. Not for years now, though."

"Where did it come from?"

"Oh, it's been in our family for a very long time."

"Do you know why the guy from that library in New York called it a Hawthorne broom?"

She considered. "Hawthorne . . . I don't think we're related to any Hawthornes. It's possible, of course, but I've never heard of any. Corys, Feltons, even an Usher. Toogoods, of course."

"But Cousin Hepzibah—" I didn't even really know what to ask. "What is it about our family? I mean, ghosts and buried treasure and flying broomsticks . . ."

"It's true. Our family has some unusual history," she said. "But I think most families do, if you look far enough back—or far enough forward. The world is a very strange place."

I couldn't disagree, especially after everything that had happened since we moved to the Thorne Mansion.

"Now that I think of it, though," Cousin Hepzibah went on, "have you ever read Nathaniel Hawthorne, the mid-nineteenth-century author? We're not related to him, as far as I know, but he has characters named Cory and Felton in some of his stories. I wonder if there's any connection."

"You mean he knew our family, and that's where he got the inspiration for those stories? He wrote about us?"

"I don't know. Maybe. The Ushers, too . . . they're not in any Hawthorne books, but there's 'The Fall of the House of Usher,' that famous short story by Edgar Allan Poe."

"I wonder whether Laetitia Flint knew our family too," I said. "Lately I've been feeling like I'm living in a Flint novel, with all the ghosts and crows and bats and cliffs."

"She may well have known the Thornes," said Cousin Hepzibah. "And I often feel that way myself."

We started our sheep-heart lab that week. The thing reeked of formaldehyde and squirted when you squeezed it—or, to be more precise, when Cole squeezed it—but it was pretty fascinating, actually. I loved the system of valves and chambers.

"Quit it, Cole," I said. "You're getting disgusting heart juice all over everything."

"I'm just demonstrating the pump action! See how it comes out the aorta?"

A spray of liquid pattered on Dolores's notebook. "Hey!" She scrubbed at it with a paper towel.

"Sorry, Lola." He flashed his white-toothed smile at her, and she smiled back indulgently.

Why does everybody melt when he does that? I sliced into the heart with my scalpel, biting my tongue and thinking of all the jokes I could make about heart attacks and heartbreak.

CHAPTER ELEVEN

Hepzibah Toogood's Story

A few days later, I came home from practicing my flying skills to find a visitor in the parlor drinking tea with Cousin Hepzibah, his back to me.

"Oh, there you are, Sukie," said Cousin Hepzibah. "Your friend's here."

My friend?

The guest turned around. It was Cole Farley. "Hi, Sp— Hi, Sukie!" he said, grinning.

"Cole! What are you doing here?"

"I brought your lab book—you left it in class. Your cousin's been telling me about your family."

"I'll just get you a cup of tea, child," offered Cousin Hepzibah, leaning forward and feeling for her cane.

Cole put a hand on her arm. "No, you sit still, Miss Thorne." He crossed the room to the china cabinet and took out a third cup and saucer. The cups were tiny white things without handles, as thin as eggshells, painted with little black flowers.

"No need to be so formal, dear. You can call me Hepzibah.

I know, it's a mouthful. They used to call me Eppie when I was a girl."

"Eppie!" I said. I couldn't quite picture it.

Cousin Hepzibah nodded. "You never called your sister Hepzibah Eppie?"

"No, just Kitty. Occasionally Happy, but only when she was in a very bad mood."

"How do you get Kitty from Hepzibah?" asked Cole.

"Hepzibah, Hepcat, Kitty," I explained.

"What's a hepcat? Is that like a hellcat?" He didn't wait for an answer. "It's so awesome—your cousin was just telling me about how your great-great-great-great-great-great-great-great-great-grandfather was a pirate!" He rattled off the *greats* like a marble bouncing down stairs.

"Not our many-greats-grandfather, child, just our many-greats-uncle," said Cousin Hepzibah.

"Oh, right. The many-greats-grandfather was the witch, right?"

Cousin Hepzibah nodded. "Accused. His accuser recanted and died the night before the execution, and the magistrate set our ancestor free. He lived the rest of his life under a shadow."

I groaned inwardly. A witch! Now Cole would never, ever stop calling me Spooky. "Tell me about the pirate," I said. "You mentioned him before, but you never really told me the whole story," I said.

"You don't know about your pirate uncle? Tell her, Hepzibah!" said Cole.

Cousin Hepzibah took a long swig of tea, put down her cup, and began.

• • •

"It was way back in the eighteenth century. This house had passed into the hands of Obadiah Thorne, a wealthy ship owner. Obadiah had no sons, only two daughters, Hepzibah and Obedience—Windy and Beedie, they were called."

"Obedience? That's a weird name," said Cole.

"Not really, not back then. Lots of babies had names like that—Prudence and Experience and Preserved. Their mother was Patience. If Beedie had been a son, they would have called her Obadiah Junior, and Obedience sounds pretty close."

"I guess so," said Cole.

"Patience was a pretty, pale, delicate little thing," Cousin Hepzibah went on. "Giving birth to Obedience almost killed her. Obadiah didn't think she would have any more children, so Obedience was the closest he would come to having a son named after him."

"Did she?" I asked. "Their mother. Have any more children."

"Sadly, no. She died of a fever when Windy was twelve and Beedie only five. An elderly cousin, Annabel Thorne, came to look after the little girls. When the weather was good, they used to sit on the widow's walk under an awning, sewing their samplers and watching the sails come up over the horizon. There's Beedie's sampler, hanging over the card table."

I crossed the parlor to examine it more closely. A border of faded red yarn roses twined around a background of plain brownish linen. In the center stood a house with one gigantic black wool crow perched on the left chimney and another about to land on the right one. The chimneys didn't look big enough to hold them. Above the crows flew a fleet of ships with tiny white sails. The ships were the same size as the birds, and the left-hand crow glared at them with his cross-stitched eye, as if warning them to stay off his roof.

Under the house stood a man in a yellow coat, a white-haired old lady, two little girls with pointy shoes showing under their dresses, and a little dog, who was sniffing at a capital *A*. The rest of the alphabet followed in tidy rows of capital and lowercase letters, each a different color. It looked as though a family of gardeners was getting ready to weed its letter patch.

In an oval frame at the bottom, I read the verse. "Obedience Thorne is my name & with my Needle I wrought the same." Apparently Beedie had embroidered the frame first and run out of space; the *me* of *same* spilled out.

"Is this a real house?" asked Cole, pointing.

"Of course! That's *this* house, before they built most of the additions," said Cousin Hepzibah.

"Wow, that's so cool!" I wondered whether the crows on the roof were the ancestors of the ones that cawed outside my window.

"What about Windy's sampler?" I asked. "Do you have that one, too?"

"She never finished it. She had no discipline, that aunt of ours. That's how she got her nickname—she was always gusting off in different directions. Until she met Phineas Toogood, that is."

"The pirate?"

"Not at first. He was an honest sailor when they met—second mate on one of Obadiah's ships, the *Sandpiper.* Obadiah sent the girls and Miss Annabel on the *Sandpiper* to visit cousins in Portland the summer Windy was seventeen. When Windy's little dog, Tiber, was swept off deck in a swell, Phinny Toogood dived in and rescued him. That was how it began.

"Whenever the *Sandpiper* docked in North Harbor, Phinny would find a way to see Windy. He brought her gifts—a Chinese comb, a South Sea shell, a thimble he carved from the tip of a walrus tusk, with "*Sandpiper*" scribed in black and their initials twined together. She gave him a silk handkerchief that she'd embroidered with a dolphin. That was the first sewing project she managed to finish, so you can imagine how she must have loved him.

"Phinny and Windy agreed to marry as soon as Phinny had saved up enough to build a little house in Newport. But Obadiah had other plans for his daughter. He wanted his property to stay in the hands of the Thornes. A second cousin of Obadiah's, Japhet Thorne, had inherited the adjoining parcel—that's the land between the carriage house and the bottom of the hill where your school bus stops. Obadiah ordered Windy to marry Japhet and forget Phinny.

"Japhet was considered an excellent catch. He was tall and handsome, with good manners, if a little stiff. He had plenty of money. But Windy didn't like him, and she loved Phinny. She told her father she would rather stay single her whole life long. He threatened to cut her off without a shilling, but she told him she didn't care.

"Then one Sunday Phinny had a friend slip a note into Windy's prayer book at church, telling her the little house was ready and he was waiting for her in the village. That night she climbed out her window. They were married in the little white church on Oak Street, the one next to that new yoga place. They exchanged silver rings engraved with the motto 'Your Heart is my Home.'

"When her father heard the news, he fell back into his chair, twitching and clutching at his throat. Miss Annabel sent for the doctor, who bled Obadiah and put him to bed. With careful nursing, he recovered somewhat, but his right side was paralyzed and he never spoke again."

"Was it a stroke?" Cole asked.

"Yes, an apoplectic fit, the doctor said. That's what they called strokes back then. Beedie wrote to her sister begging her to come home, but Windy responded that if the news of her marriage had half killed her father, the sight of her wedding ring would likely finish him off.

"A few months later, though, Beedie wrote again and this time Windy came. Phinny had shipped out as first mate on the schooner *Oracle*, and Windy was lonely in the little house without him. Besides, by then she was expecting a child. She wanted to be near her family.

"When her father saw her so round and rosy, the left side of his mouth lifted in half a smile and he reached out his left hand, the tears streaming down his face. Windy threw herself into his arms, weeping. But she had been right to worry: The joy of the reconciliation was too much for the old man. He didn't live long enough to hold his grandson.

"They say little Jack was a fat, smiling baby, with his mother's blue eyes and his father's black hair. His aunt Beedie, who had only recently put away her dolls and started wearing long skirts like a lady, couldn't get enough of him. She sewed him bonnets and dresses and fed him his porridge with her own little spoon.

"Although Obadiah had threatened to change his will, his apoplexy had robbed him of speech before he'd had time to call for his lawyer. Except for Beedie's dowry and a handful of bequests to servants, Windy inherited everything: the Thorne Mansion, the land it stood on, everything in it, the ships, and the money.

"Japhet Thorne was beside himself with rage when he heard. From his bedroom window, he could look up the hill to the grand house that he'd believed would be his. Now not only had his promised bride married someone else, but the Thorne Mansion would pass out of Thorne hands.

"So Japhet sought out the infamous Captain Tempest of the *Pretty Polly*, the most notorious pirate on the coast, and offered him a hundred pounds in gold to kill Windy's husband, Phineas, and bring his head back as proof.

"Red Tom Tempest readily agreed. 'A proposition worthy of the *Polly*,' laughed Red Tom, showing off his three gold teeth. They sealed their bargain with rum."

I objected. "Wait, hang on! What's this Red Tom Tempest person doing in the story? I thought *Phinny* was supposed to be the pirate!"

Cousin Hepzibah patted my hand. "I'm getting there, dear."

"There can be more than one pirate, silly," said Cole. "Me hearties," he added as an afterthought.

Cousin Hepzibah continued, "The storms were strong that year, and many a fortune was smashed into driftwood up and down the coast. News came that the *Oracle* had gone down with all hands. Phineas Toogood was no more.

"Japhet went to his cousin and asked her again to marry him. 'A widow needs a protector and a boy needs a father,' he said. But Windy refused to believe her husband was really dead. 'My boy *has* a father,' she told Japhet.

"Then word came—from a trader who had heard a story in a tavern on Jamaica—that what had sunk the *Oracle* was not a storm, but pirates.

"Windy maintained that no pirates would kill such a fine sailor. They must have taken him prisoner to help sail their ship, she insisted. Phinny would escape and come home to her.

"When Japhet heard this he waited eagerly for Red Tom Tempest to deliver on his promise and bring him Phinny's head. But when the pirate captain finally came, he brought bad news. Though wounded, Phineas had escaped on the *Oracle*'s lifeboat. 'But I did bring you this,' said Red Tom, handing Japhet a small brandy cask."

"What was in it?" asked Cole, bouncing in his chair and spilling a little tea into his saucer.

"I'm just getting to that," said Cousin Hepzibah. "Japhet brought the cask to Windy. He told her, 'I'm afraid I have some painful news. A sailor of my acquaintance has a brother who is cook aboard the *Pretty Polly*. He saw your husband fall in the fight, mortally wounded. It grieves me to tell you that the pirates threw him overboard and the cook saw a pair of sharks fighting over his body. Nothing remains of him but this.' He handed Windy the cask. 'I deeply regret the pain this must be causing you, but I know that unless you see it with your own eyes, you will persist in your unfortunate refusal to accept your husband's demise.'

"Windy opened the cask, shrieked, and fell back in a swoon. Inside the cask was Phinny's left hand, pickled in brandy. She couldn't mistake it—it was wearing the wedding ring that she had given him."

Cole and I spoke at once.

"Cool!" he said.

"Eww!" I said.

"What did Windy do then?" I asked.

"At last she believed Japhet that Phinny was dead. She buried his hand in the little graveyard at the top of the hill—you can still see the gravestone, the one with the rose climbing on it. She fell into a decline. The only thing that would bring her out of herself was little Jack, who had grown into a fine, strong child.

"Now that Phinny was out of the way, Japhet hoped she would be persuaded to marry him. It was what her father had wanted, after all. But little Jack still stood between him and the Thorne property. So he waited until one day, when old Cousin Annabel, who was watching the little boy, had nodded into a doze. The little boy was never seen again after that day. Japhet told Windy little Jack had wandered off and fallen from the cliff into the sea. 'I saw him at the edge, and then I saw him slip. I ran, but I was too late to catch him,' he told Windy.

"That's horrible!" I said.

"Then what happened?" Cole asked.

"Beedie tried to comfort her sister, but it was no use. Windy spent her days and nights on the widow's walk, pale as a ghost, staring at the sea, as if she hoped to see her husband's sails come up over the horizon. Then, one morning, they found her body under the widow's walk, her neck broken."

"Did she throw herself off? Did Japhet push her?" I asked.

"Nobody knows how she fell. They called it an accident and buried her in the little graveyard beside her husband's hand. After Beedie had mourned for three years, Japhet convinced her to marry him. So he got the Thorne property after all."

"Wait! What are you saying?" I asked, horrified. "You mean *Japhet* is our great-great-whatever-great-*grandfather*? That *murderer*?"

"That's right," said Cousin Hepzibah. "And that's when our family started losing children. Japhet's son, Japhet Junior, was the first to die of the Thorne blood disease. They say it's a punishment for his crimes."

"But that's not *fair*!" I said. "Why should my sister die because of him? Kitty didn't murder anyone!"

Cousin Hepzibah squeezed my hand. "I know. It isn't fair," she said.

After an awkward pause, Cole asked, "But what happened to Phineas? You said he was a pirate?"

Cousin Hepzibah sighed. "He and his shipmates washed up on an island, where they were taken in by a colony of Africans who had survived the wreck of a slave ship."

"This story is getting very complicated," I said. It reminded me of one of those long, winding Laetitia Flint ghost stories I'd been reading on the bus. Cousin Hepzibah liked those books too—and it crossed my mind that maybe some of the details had found their way into her story. Or maybe she was right, and our family had inspired old writers.

"Of course. Nothing about our family is ever simple," said Cousin Hepzibah. She continued, "After Phinny's arm had healed, he determined to return home to Windy. But when sailors brought word of her death, he decided to avenge himself on Red Tom Tempest. With the help of his old shipmates and his new friends, he captured the *Pretty Polly*, made Captain Tempest walk the plank, and turned his hand to piracy himself. He and his friends were picky about which ships they stopped, though—they preyed only on slavers. They would pocket the valuables and set the cargo free."

"How did he capture the *Polly*? And how do you know all this?" I asked.

"Family lore," said Cousin Hepzibah. "And there's a lot written about it in the family papers."

"But if Phinny was still alive, why didn't he inherit the Thorne Mansion?" I asked. "Why did it go to Beedie and Japhet?"

"Japhet had connections. He got his magistrate friend to declare Phinny dead on the strength of the hand and Tom Tempest's account. Besides, Phinny was a pirate, an outlaw. If he ever did come home, he never showed his face."

"What happened to his treasure?" asked Cole.

"Nobody knows anything for sure," said my cousin. "Just rumors."

"What's the treasure supposed to be? Jewels? Pieces of eight?"

She shrugged. "All I know is the story: There's supposed to

be hidden treasure," said my cousin. "Maybe even a map. Nobody's ever found either one, though."

"Can we look?" Cole flashed his magic smile at Cousin Hepzibah.

"Please do—I hope you find it. Sukie, dear, why don't you show Cole around?"

"Right now? It's almost dinnertime, and I have a lot of homework," I said.

"Next time, then," said my cousin, holding out her hand to Cole. "It was lovely to meet you, child. Come again soon."

"Thanks, I will. I can't wait to see more of this house. I always knew it would be cool in here, but I had no idea *how* cool."

"I'll show you out," I said.

"What are you doing here *really*, Cole?" I asked as soon as we were out of the room. "Are you after Cousin Hepzibah's treasure?"

"Depends what you mean by *after.* You said your family needed money. If we find it, you could get a phone and we could text each other like normal people. Maybe you could even buy back your old house."

The thought made me ache with longing, as if someone was squeezing formaldehyde through my own heart. "Except it's *Cousin Hepzibah's* treasure, if it even exists."

"I bet she would use it to help you, though. She seems really nice. You sure we don't have time for a little look around before I go?"

"Sorry."

"All right, see you in the morning, then. Oh, wait." He dug in his book bag and pulled out my lab notebook. "Better take care of this. Ms. Pitch would kill us if we lose all that data—we only get one heart."

"I like your friend," said Cousin Hepzibah when I came back. "What a thoughtful young man. Handsome, too, and so fond of you."

"Fond of *me*?"

"Of course. Didn't he come out of his way to return your notebook? He says he's been making better grades in science since you became his lab partner."

"He told you that? I don't know, Cousin Hepzibah. I'm not sure I trust him. He and his friends used to call me names and throw food at me in the cafeteria. They didn't stop until Kitty gave them food poisoning. She really doesn't like him."

Cousin Hepzibah shrugged. "Well, that's ghosts. They can't change, so they don't understand when the living do."

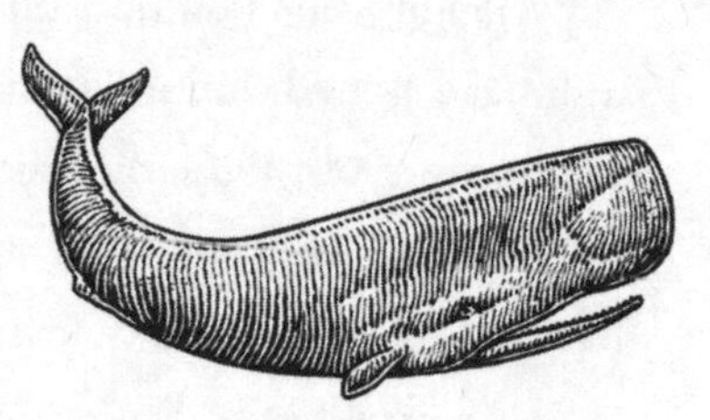

CHAPTER TWELVE

The Thorne Mansion Library

I spent the next few afternoons after school searching the Thorne Mansion library for clues to Hepzibah Toogood's treasure.

The library was a large, dark room that was lined floor to ceiling with bookcases. Ladders rolled along a railing so you could reach the upper shelves. A pair of old armchairs covered in cracked green leather flanked the fireplace, and inlaid cabinets guarded the windows, making deep nooks for window seats. With a few more lamps and a lot less dust, I thought, I could make it into a very inviting room.

I found a pair of table lamps made from Chinese vases in the attic and brought them downstairs. They threw cozy circles of light.

My Thorne ancestors loved to read everything, apparently: sermons, essays, and poetry, but especially fiction. They favored American writers. Their shelves were crammed with multivolume sets of Hawthorne, Melville, and Poe, Washington Irving and Laetitia Flint, James Fenimore Cooper and Harriet Beecher Stowe, bound in leather or faded crimson cloth. Some looked old enough to be first editions. I checked to see if any of the authors had signed them—if Cousin Hepzibah was right and they wrote some of their stories about our family, maybe they were friends of our ancestors. A signature might make a book even more valuable. But I didn't find any signed copies.

I did find something much more exciting, though: One whole bookcase held diaries! The Thorne ladies had filled volume after volume with their faded, spidery descriptions of apple harvests and new bonnets, steamship jaunts to Providence, toothaches, baby nieces, and recipes for arrack punch. Reading the diaries gave me a strange thrill—it was like traveling back in time and talking to my own ancestors!

I pulled volumes off the shelves and opened them at random, getting lost in the stories. Theodosia Thorne, the lady who presided over the expansion of the outbuildings in the 1830s, had strong opinions about horses: Her favorite mare was Scheherazade, a white Arabian, and her favorite carriage horses were called Twilight and Novalis. I remembered seeing a painting of a white horse in the gun room—I wondered if that could be Scheherazade.

But Windy had lived long before the 1830s. I combed the shelves for older volumes. In the 1790s, Miss Mary Thorne accompanied her brother John on a trip to the Far East, where she greatly admired the shape of the pagoda roofs and brought back a set of porcelain from Canton—maybe the very teacups we'd just been drinking from.

Even the 1790s was too late for Windy, though. I made myself put down Miss Mary's account of a typhoon east of Japan to search the rest of the room.

I couldn't find any diaries by Windy or Beedie, so I opened the fancy secretary desk beside the door. I found a bundle of family papers there, and a lot more in the cabinets by the windows: wills and deeds and account ledgers and endless bundles of letters tied up with cloth tape. It was overwhelming. Where would I even begin?

Notes in the big leather-bound Bible and a calligraphic family tree drawn by some 1880s Thorne confirmed the outlines of Cousin Hepzibah's story. Squinting at the doves and curlicues and trumpet-blaring cherubs, I read that Obadiah Thorne and his wife—Patience, née Cloyse—had had two daughters, Hepzibah and Obedience; Hepzibah had married Phineas Toogood and Obedience had married her second cousin, Japhet Thorne; Hepzibah Toogood and her young son, John, had died within a month of each other, not long after Phineas; and Thornes in every subsequent generation died young. The Bible and the family tree had nothing to say about murders or buried treasure, however.

I brought a few volumes of diaries upstairs that night to read in bed. Miss Mary had started keeping hers when she was just a girl, only nine, and the way she took care of John, her little brother, reminded me of Kitty. She wrote about him impatiently, complaining about how he pushed through the bushes to get to the blackberries and tore his new "frock," the one she had just finished sewing. "He made me eat all the Ripest fruit, pushing them between my Lips. He stained my Collar with juice. He is a Naughty, Naughty little Love, and I am very Vex't with him."

That sounded like Kitty complaining about me. She used to scrub my scraped knees with alcohol wipes. "Ow, Kitty! That stings!" I would wail, trying to twist away.

"Stand still! You're getting blood all over me. You'll get an infection if I don't clean that."

"I don't care!"

"Well, I do. What if your legs fall off and I have to carry you everywhere? Stop crying! I was just kidding, your legs aren't really going to fall off, because you're going to stand still and let me finish. Anyway, I don't really mind carrying you, as long as it's not very far. If I sing you the nut tree song, will you stop howling?" And she would slap a Band-Aid on my knee, hug me impatiently and a little too hard, and sing my favorite nursery rhyme, the one about the nut tree and the princess and the golden pear.

"Thorne girls take good care of their siblings," I told the air. "Listen to this." I read the passage about the frock and the blackberries out loud. Kitty wasn't completely present right then—not present enough to understand the words—but I felt *something*, so I thought she might be nearby. She would probably get the gist.

I could have summoned her with the whistle, but I almost never did that nowadays. She came too often as it was. I had a feeling that the more I used the whistle, the thinner I would make the barrier between her world and mine. What if it wore away to nothing?

When I got to the later sections in Miss Mary's diary, though—the parts when she wrote about sailing to China on grown-up John's ship—I felt a presence much more sinister than Kitty's or Windy's. The back of my neck prickled. It felt more like that second presence from the other night, the hard, oppressive presence that had chased Windy off.

"Who are you?" I asked the air.

Nobody answered.

"Go away, then!"

Nobody answered again. But nobody left, either.

"Okay, stay, then. Whatever. I'm a Thorne—you can't scare me. I belong here."

I hoped it was true. It didn't really feel true, whatever Cousin Hepzibah said.

That night dreams chopped my sleep into a zillion pieces. I dreamed about severed hands and dead Thorne kids, about lost wills and storms at sea. That hard presence haunted all my dreams.

CHAPTER THIRTEEN
Fashion Advice

School lunch on Friday was Mystery Stew, which was bad enough. Becky and Hannah Lee made it worse by pointing at my ankles. Looking down, I saw that the gap between my jeans hem and my shoes had widened to show way more sock than was considered proper in North Harbor society.

These were the last clothes I had left from Kitty. I remembered how much I hated having to wear Kitty's hand-me-downs when I was little. I wanted something new, something of my own, especially in colors that looked good on a pale blonde, not a rosy redhead. Then, after she died, her clothes were all I wanted to wear. They made me feel she was hugging me.

Hugging me pretty tightly, these days. I was taller now than she'd ever been, and the waistband was starting to pinch. I knew I'd been growing, but I hadn't realized it had gotten so bad. Spring might be on its way, but it was still far too cold out to just turn my jeans into cutoffs.

It's not that the snickering bothered *me*. But I worried what would happen if Becky and Hannah got Kitty riled up. She never liked it when people laughed at me, and I didn't think she would react too well to having her jeans mocked, either.

I was scanning the chaotic cafeteria for an empty seat far away from the snickerers when I heard my name. Dolores Pereira waved me over to the table where she was sitting with her cousin Amanda.

"Ask her, Lola," said Amanda, giggling.

"No, you ask her," said Lola. "You're the one who wants to know."

"Ask me about what?"

"Go on, Amanda!" said Lola.

"You've been hanging out with Cole Farley, right?" said Amanda.

"Uh, yeah. I guess," I said.

"What's his family like? Is his brother as cute as he is?"

"I don't know. I haven't met his family," I said.

"See? I told you," said Lola to her cousin. "What do you think of Cole, though?" she asked me.

"He's okay. When he's not being obnoxious."

"How's he obnoxious?" asked Amanda.

"He's always calling me names, for one thing."

"I wish he would call *me* names," said Amanda.

"I'm sure he'd be happy to. Want me to tell him?" I offered.

"What do you want him to call you? Amanda Panda? Amanda Banana?" Lola asked.

Amanda dissolved in giggles and buried her head in Lola's shoulder. When she recovered, she said, "Hey, I like your hair thing. Where'd you get it?"

I felt my head. I was wearing a hair clip with tatted lace that

Cousin Hepzibah had given me. I took it out and handed it to her. "My cousin. She made it for me."

"Really? Who's your cousin? Does she go to school here?" asked Amanda.

I laughed. "No, she's, like, ninety years old!"

"That's really cool. Can I see it?" said Lola, taking the clip.

"Could she make me one?" asked Amanda.

"I can ask," I said. "Or I could ask her to show me how."

"If she teaches you, would you teach me?" asked Lola.

"Sure." I put the clip back in my hair.

"You know who I think is *really* cute? Garvin Graves," said Amanda.

Lola and I made faces.

"You're kidding!" I said.

Lola said, "Garvin *Graves*? He's *awful*!"

"How's he awful?"

"He's mean," said Lola.

"You can be mean and still be cute," said Amanda. "Look at those arms!"

"Stay away from those arms," said Lola. "Hey, Sukie, did you figure out Ms. Pitch's extra-credit problem from yesterday?"

"No, I haven't really worked on it yet. Did you?"

She shook her head.

"What is it? Maybe I can figure it out," said Amanda.

The problem was about strategies for winning the student-council elections in various scenarios, with different percentages of the vote required for avoiding a runoff. Lola and I worked on it together for a while, even though Amanda thought there was no point.

"Who cares? Hannah Lee's going to win no matter what," she said.

The end-of-lunch warning bell rang, and we crumpled up our food wrappers. "Hey, can I ask you guys something? Are my pants too short?" I asked.

"Stand up," said Lola. "Now turn around." She shook her head regretfully. "Yeah, definitely too short."

Amanda nodded. "Those are some serious high waters."

"Thanks, I was afraid you'd say that."

Too bad. I would have to spend what was left of my birthday money on new pants.

Still, it was nice to have someone who would tell me straight out, instead of just snickering behind my back. It felt almost like having friends.

We ran into Cole when we went to dump our trays in the trash. "Howdy, partners," he said.

"Howdy to you too, Cole," said Lola. "Hey, my cousin has a question for you." She nudged Amanda.

Amanda giggled and fake-slapped her. "I do not!"

"Yes, she does. It's about your brother."

"Jake? What about him?" asked Cole.

"Nothing," said Amanda.

Lola said, "Amanda wanted to know, is he—"

Amanda jumped in quickly, talking over Lola. "I wanted to know, is he . . . um, is he on a sports team?"

"Yeah, he plays hockey. He's pretty good too. Why?"

"I don't know, I just . . ." Amanda looked like she wished she could die.

To spare her from having to answer, I said, "Are you athletic too, Cole? What about the rest of your family?"

Cole said, "My dad and my grandfather both played football in high school. And some of my ancestors way back were pretty good at sports—at least, they won races and stuff at church picnics. I don't think they had sports teams back then."

"Wow—how do you know all that?" asked Amanda.

"My grandpa kept the ribbons they won. He loves that kind of thing, like history. He has a lot of old family letters. Most of them are just about boring stuff like who owes them money or what the pastor said at church. But some of the men were sailors, and their letters are pretty cool. They sailed all over the world, to China and India and places like that."

Hannah and Becky came over with their sandwich wrappers. "Is this the new hot spot—the trash?" said Becky.

"That's right," said Cole. "It's where everyone who's anyone dumps their trays."

Becky glanced at my ankles again, but she didn't say anything out loud. Apparently there were some advantages to having Cole as a friend.

CHAPTER FOURTEEN

Adolphus T. Feathertop, Factor-at-Large

Even though Cole's presence kept the girls from giving me a hard time about my pants, the high water situation was dire. I got my birthday money out of its hiding place—an old cocoa box—and asked Dad to take me to the shopping center in East Harbor.

"Sure, but I have to swing by a couple of house sales this afternoon," said Dad. "We'll stop there after."

"Okay." Maybe I might even find some decent clothes for cheap at the house sales.

The first house was a washout—just a lot of baby clothes and car seats—but the second looked promising. An elderly widow had died, and her niece was selling everything: furniture, linens, kitchen stuff, clothing. Some of the furniture had been in the family for generations; judging from the hall tree and the breakfront, they'd been pretty well off in the 1880s. And the old lady had taken good care of her clothes. There were even a few pairs of jeans in a style I remembered Grandma O'Dare wearing.

I fingered a green wool dress trimmed in yellow. It came with a matching jacket with big, cheerful yellow buttons. Hannah and Becky were going to make fun of me no matter what I wore, so why not try something fun?

Then I remembered Kitty. If Hannah and Becky gave me a hard time, what would *she* do? Maybe something worse than making them sprain their ankles, even. I put the dress back.

"That was a favorite of Aunt Catherine's," said the widow's niece. "I have such a vivid image of her wearing it at Thanksgiving, with a little corsage of yellow chrysanthemums. It would look nice on you. It matches your hair. You have the height for it, too."

"I like it, but I wouldn't have anywhere to wear it. Definitely not to school," I said.

"No, I guess not. It's too formal for you young people." She held out a shoebox full of glittery brooches. "Do you like costume jewelry? Aunt Catherine had quite a bit. I know it's popular with girls nowadays."

Not at my school, but it seemed rude to say so. "Thanks." I poked around in the box politely. I wasn't really interested in costume jewelry, but I did know that some pieces could be pretty valuable. I wasn't sure I would be able to tell which were which, though. I found a big purple plastic daisy pin that I kind of liked and an iridescent rhinestone earring that Kitty would have loved. As I rummaged through the box looking for its mate, I felt a jolt so cold and evil that I stopped breathing.

I snatched my hand away and stared at the box in horror. My first impulse was to drop it and run. But then I smelled dense, chocolaty-sulfuric pipe smoke that I recognized at once. The little man who'd tried to buy my broom—was *he* here?

Without any help from me, my mind started leaping to all sorts of conclusions. The fancy-dressed pipe smoker was after whatever horror was hiding among the jewelry, it decided. And letting him get his hands on it would be a bad idea.

The widow's niece was looking at me funny. "Are you okay?"

"What? Oh, yes, sorry. I'm fine. I just stabbed myself with a pin." I needed to find whatever had given me that cold horror, but I couldn't seem to make myself reach inside the box again. Instead, I said, "Your aunt had great taste in jewelry. I'd like to buy the whole box."

The niece beamed at me. "I'm so glad! Aunt Catherine would love to know her collection has found a good home. Shall we say forty dollars? There's some good pieces in there. Some Trifari, I think."

I counted my money. "I only have thirty-seven," I said. "Plus some change."

"That's fine—you can give me thirty-five. I know Aunt Catherine would have liked you to have it."

I handed her the crumpled bills. "Thank you."

The sulfurous smoke got louder, and a man came into the room. I was right—it was the guy from the flea market. This time he was wearing a navy-blue suit with thin red pinstripes and the same red hat as last time, the one with a feather in it. "Excuse me, may I see that box?" He reached for it.

I snatched it back. "I'm sorry, I just bought it."

He turned to the widow's niece. "How much did she pay? I'll give you double."

"I'm sorry, but it's sold," she said.

"Triple, then."

"I just told you, it's sold. And I would appreciate it if you didn't smoke in my aunt's house. It's disrespectful."

He turned to me. "Will you take a hundred dollars?"

"No," I said. "It's not for sale."

"Five hundred."

"Do you even know what's inside?" I asked.

"Do you?"

I'll admit I was tempted. Five hundred dollars might not get us our house back, but it would buy a lot of jeans. But the cold touch of whatever had brushed my hand was still coursing down my spine. "I'm keeping it," I told him firmly.

He took a deep breath of smoke and released it.

"If you won't put out your pipe, I'm going to have to ask you to leave," said the widow's niece.

He took a step toward me, drawing on his pipe, his eyes flaring like the lit tobacco. I felt panic rising. What was he going to do? Where was Kitty? I scrabbled in my pocket for her whistle. There! I brought it to my lips and blew.

Kitty arrived in a dark gust of wind that sent a stack of magazines slithering to the floor and dimmed the spark in the man's pipe. She hovered a few feet up and loomed over him, her red hair writhing like snakes of flame. I'd never seen her look so impressive, so threatening. She even scared *me*.

But the scariest thing was, the man could *see* her.

Nobody ever sees Kitty—nobody except me. But the pipe-smoking clotheshorse did. He cringed, sheltering his pipe behind his hands. His face and posture seemed to crumple. Then he pulled himself together and stood up straight. He handed me a card. "If you change your mind," he said and swept out.

Kitty swept after him like an avenging orange cloud.

"I wonder what that was about," said the woman.

She couldn't mean Kitty, could she? But no—she sounded too calm. Way calmer than I was.

I took a deep breath—the remains of the smoke made me cough—and looked at the card. It read *Adolphus T. Feathertop, Factor-at-Large* and gave a phone number and an email address.

I went to the door to catch my breath and make sure he was gone. I looked up and down the street. No sign of the man, or of my sister. I went back inside.

"Did that man know your aunt? Maybe he saw her wearing a valuable brooch or something?" I asked.

"I guess that's possible. Aunt Catherine set store by her jewelry."

I felt bad, making the widow's niece pass up all that money from Adolphus T. Feathertop. It's not like I actually wanted any of the jewelry. "If I find out any of this is worth a lot, I could bring it back," I offered.

"No, don't do that," she said. "A bargain is a bargain. I would far rather you have Aunt Catherine's treasures than that rude man."

"Well, thank you. That's very nice of you."

Dad came back from loading the hall tree into the truck. Good antique hall trees always sell fast in Brooklyn, which is long on Victorian brownstones and short on coat closets. "Ready, Sukie? Let's go get you your new jeans," he said.

"Change of plans," I said. "I just spent all my money." I held up the box, lifting the lid so he could see inside.

"Jewelry? Really? Well, your money, your choice," said Dad. He gave the widow's niece a raised-eyebrows "Girls!" look that I found deeply unfair.

She glanced at my legs. "You do seem to have outgrown your slacks. Wait there." She bustled out of the room and came back with an armload of grandmother jeans, with a few pairs of woolen trousers thrown in. "These should fit. You're just about Aunt Catherine's height, maybe a bit slimmer, but you can always take them in."

What was I going to do with grandmother pants? But she had been so nice. I thanked her and followed Dad out to the truck, sniffing for sulfur. To my relief, the wind had blown away every trace of Adolphus T. Feathertop.

When we got home, I took my shoebox of jewelry up to my room, poured it out on my bed, and began to put the pieces back in the box one by one. Maybe I could sell them online. If only Cousin Hepzibah had an Internet connection.

Some of the pieces were elegant, some garish, but none gave me that cold jolt of horror when I touched them. I set aside a few nice ones: the purple enamel daisy; the earrings that reminded me of Kitty; a delicate, lacy metal bracelet I thought Amanda would like; and a blue-green rhinestone necklace the same color as a sweater of Lola's.

Would I be bribing the Pereiras to be my friends? Did that

make me a bad person? But wasn't all friendship an exchange anyway—would it be so wrong for the exchange to involve jewelry? The nice lady had been so certain her aunt Catherine would have liked the idea of me wearing her treasures. Surely she would like it even better if three of us wore them.

I reached for another brooch. As I touched it, the cold feeling swept over me like a breaking wave, pulling me under and pelting me with pebbles of stinging terror. I sank to my knees, gasping. It took everything I had to make myself open my hand and look at it rather than hurl it as far away as possible.

It was a small clasp made of onyx inlaid with gold, in a style that was popular at the end of the nineteenth century. I'd seen hundreds of pieces like that at flea markets, black stone with gold initials. In old photos, ladies wore them to hold their collars together and men used them as tie clips.

The only odd thing about the clasp was the letter itself, which was definitely not from our alphabet. It didn't look Greek or Russian, either. Not Arabic or Hebrew, not Chinese, Japanese, Korean, or Thai. Definitely not Egyptian. It looked—well, it looked foreign. Beyond foreign. Inhuman.

I didn't want to hold it. I didn't want it in my room. I didn't want it in my *life*.

Shuddering, I dropped it into a plastic bag, zipped the bag shut, and folded it up in paper. I tucked it into an empty mint tin, clicked the tin shut, started to put it in my pocket, then stopped. I zipped it into my backpack instead.

Kitty was back. She didn't like the thing. She didn't want me to keep it. She thought I should fly my broomstick far out over the ocean and toss it.

I imagined the relief I would feel as it left my hand, the splash it would make. I imagined it vanishing into the water. I imagined the currents dragging it back and forth, through seaweed and schools of fish, washing it up on a beach. I imagined someone finding it: Adolphus T. Feathertop, or—worse—some kid my age. I imagined a kid opening the box, unfolding the sodden paper, unzipping the plastic, and pinning the clasp to their jacket.

I couldn't imagine what would happen next.

Something bad.

I needed help. I dug out Elizabeth Rew's card with the address of the New-York Circulating Material Repository. I put on my parka, grabbed my backpack with the clasp in it, took the Hawthorne broom up to the widow's walk, swung my leg over, and launched myself out into the air, swiveling toward the sea and heading down the coast.

CHAPTER FIFTEEN

The New-York Circulating Material Repository

The ride to New York City took a lot longer than I expected, mostly because I hadn't thought it through. North Harbor is a couple of hundred miles from Manhattan as the crow flies. As it happened, a crow took off from one of the chimneys and flew out ahead of me, and I actually considered following it before deciding that would be insane. So I took Andre's advice from earlier and hugged the coast.

Following all the bends along the shore—all the coves and nubbles and promontories—added distance to my trip. Clinging to the broomstick with hands and knees, I urged it to go faster, faster! I outstripped crows and seagulls. Mist stung my cheeks and soaked through my scarf. Kitty hated it. This was far, far more dangerous than riding a bike without training wheels. She tried to help by blowing the air backward from my face, but that just whipped my hair around, stinging my ears. My legs were aching and everything chafed.

Then I saw a helicopter ahead of me, and I panicked. I gave the broom a storm of mixed messages: Up! Down! Forward—no, back! But most of all, *go*! *Get past it!*

The broomstick hung for a moment, as if paralyzed. The helicopter came hurtling toward me. It seemed to be blowing up like a balloon. Then something intangible snapped, and the broomstick broke loose into some unknown dimension. Everything vanished: the helicopter, the sharp mist, the seagulls, the coast. My sister. I was alone in dark, blank, racing silence.

I gasped and pulled up on the broom's end. The broom flapped impatiently, as if irritated at being interrupted by someone who clearly had no idea what she was doing.

"Take me back," I shouted. My voice sounded dim and flat in the emptiness. "Go back to the coast!"

The broom didn't respond.

"Broom! Come *on*!"

The broom made a reluctant turn—I felt the motion, but I couldn't tell the direction—and gave a swishing shudder, as if it were sweeping stars along the infinite stone wall at the end of the universe. It made a rough, sparking sound. Then I felt the air catch around my arms and legs, and the wind came back, slicing at my forehead. I blinked away tears and saw the coast below me again, laid out like a map. The helicopter was gone, as was Connecticut. I saw Manhattan ahead of me. We were almost there.

I flew slowly forward and let myself down in Central Park, choosing a wooded area that looked empty. Nobody saw me land. I staggered off the broomstick, straightening my shaking legs. I made my way out of the park near the Metropolitan Museum of Art and walked quickly through well-kept streets to the address on Elizabeth's card.

The New-York Circulating Material Repository was a townhouse at the end of a row of similar-looking houses. It had marble stairs, double doors, and a brass plaque.

Kitty found me as I was walking up the steps. She was furious. What had I done back there? Where had I disappeared to when that helicopter had shown up? Did I have any idea how fast helicopters go? What if I hadn't made it out of the way in time?

"I'm fine, Kitty," I said. "I don't think the broom wanted to get caught in those propellers any more than I did."

She was still blasting me with fury as I pulled open the heavy doors.

Inside was a surprisingly big room with a tall ceiling and a marble floor. A girl about my age was sitting at a desk, reading a book. She glanced up, smiled, then went back to her book.

I walked over to the desk. "Can I help you?" she asked in a friendly voice.

"Um, yeah, I hope so."

"First time here?"

I nodded. "I was hoping to see Dr. Rew. Is she here?"

"Yes, I think so. Is she expecting you?"

"I doubt it." Though who really knew what someone like that expected. "If she's busy, I could talk to Andre Merritt."

She raised one eyebrow, then lifted the receiver of an

old-fashioned dial telephone like the one in my tower room. "Elizabeth? You have visitors downstairs, asking for you and Andre. . . . No, a girl and . . . I'm not sure. Right, hang on." She held the mouthpiece away from her and asked, "Your name?"

"Sukie O'Dare."

She nodded, then told the telephone, "She says she's Sukie O'Dare. . . . Okay, good." She hung up the receiver. "Take the elevator up to four. Someone will meet you there. Do you want to leave that here?" She pointed to my broomstick.

"No, thanks, I'd rather keep it with me."

"That's fine. Elevator's that way."

"Thanks."

"No problem."

As the elevator doors shut behind me and Kitty, I realized the girl behind the desk had referred to us in the plural.

The elevator opened onto a landing with white walls, tile floors, and Andre Merritt. He was even taller than I remembered. "What's up, Sukie?" He nodded down at me.

I stepped out and stood there awkwardly with my broomstick and my ghost sister. "Hi, Andre."

"Laila downstairs said you want to see Libbet? Come on, I'll take you to her office." He held a door for me and strode off down a hallway. I followed him, and Kitty skimmed along on the wall beside us like a movie of herself being projected from a moving film projector. Andre kept glancing at the wall and frowning, but he didn't seem to actually see her.

"Is that what you wanted to talk about?" he asked, nodding at my broom.

"One of the things."

"Did you change your mind about selling it?"

"No! I just—I was hoping you could tell me more about it. The broom and something else I brought."

"Cool, okay. Here." We stopped in front of a narrow, arched door made of dark wood. A brass plaque read *Elizabeth Rew, Acquisitions.* Andre knocked.

"Come in," called Elizabeth.

He opened the door a crack and squeezed himself through. "Come in, Sukie," he said when I hesitated, pulling the door open a millimeter more and snaking an arm out to take my elbow.

Turning sideways and sucking in my breath, I eased myself in after him.

The tiny room was shaped like a bud vase: round, narrow, and very tall, tapering toward a distant domed skylight. A single shelf crammed with objects spiraled around the walls all the way up, with little round windows scattered here and there among the objects on the shelf. A pulley and a rope ladder dangled from an iron bar just under the skylight.

Elizabeth sat behind a desk piled with objects and teetering towers of papers. Other piles on the floor blocked the door, preventing it from opening all the way—not that there was room for it to open anyway, with Andre and me taking up all the remaining floor space.

"Welcome, welcome, Sukie," Elizabeth said. "Please, sit down."

I looked around for a chair, but there were none. Where would they even fit?

Andre laughed, reached behind me, and did something to a spot on the wall. A narrow section unfolded down into a cushioned seat. He unfolded one for himself too and sat down, his knees bumping up against Elizabeth's desk.

I unzipped my parka and unwound my scarf.

"Here, you can put those . . ." Elizabeth looked around. There really was nowhere to put them.

"That's okay. I can hold them," I said, tucking my backpack behind my legs, draping my coat over my knees, and leaning the broom against the spiral shelf. "This is quite a room!"

Elizabeth laughed. "Yeah, well, they didn't have a proper office for me when I got promoted, so they had to get creative. This used to be a chimney. So. What brings you here today?"

CHAPTER SIXTEEN

A Fictional Family

I had no idea where to start.

"I found something kind of—I don't know. I couldn't figure out what to do with it. But you seemed to know about the broom and stuff, and I thought . . ." I trailed off and began again. "Well, to start with, what *is* this broom?"

Elizabeth and Andre looked at each other. "What do you know about it already?" Elizabeth asked carefully.

"Not much, really. I know you guys call it a Hawthorne broom—I don't know why. I know people really want it, especially that creepy guy with the pipe. I know it's been in my family for generations. Cousin Hepzibah gave it to me. And I know—" I took a deep breath. But I wasn't giving away any secrets. They knew this themselves already. It's why I'd come to talk to them. "I know it can fly. I flew down here on it."

Elizabeth and Andre were nodding. "So that's why you're here? Because you discovered that flying broomsticks exist and you have one, and that's freaking you out, and you want us to tell you more about it?" said Elizabeth.

"Yes," I said. "There's something else I want to show you too, but let's start with the broom."

"Okay," said Elizabeth. "Well, obviously, what you have is a witch's broomstick. Flying broomsticks are one of the more common types of supernatural fictional objects. You find them all over, from Goethe to *The Wizard of Oz*. But judging from the age and style of yours, where your family's from, and the fact that it's been in your family for generations, we think it's probably one of the brooms from Hawthorne."

I didn't understand. "Which Hawthorne? There are lots of towns called Hawthorne. Did you mean Hawthorne, Massachusetts? Or Hawthorne, New Hampshire?"

"Not where," said Andre. "Who. Nathaniel Hawthorne, the American writer from the nineteenth century. He wrote a bunch of stories and novels about supernatural events. Some of them have witches' broomsticks in them. We think yours is one of those."

"You mean Nathaniel Hawthorne wrote about real-life magical flying broomsticks in his fiction?" I asked. "He based his stories on actual witches?" That made sense. Cousin Hepzibah had suggested that some of the old writers had gotten the names of their characters from our family; maybe they'd gotten the idea for witches' broomsticks from us, too. Did that mean my ancestors were not just pirates and ghosts, but witches, too?

Elizabeth and Andre looked at each other again. "Not exactly," said Andre. "The stories are fiction. Hawthorne made them up. What you've got is a fictional broomstick."

"No, it's not! It's real!" I picked it up and held it out to

Andre and Elizabeth. "See—feel it! It's not made up. It's solid. It really flew—it really carried me hundreds of miles."

"Well, yes. We're not denying that," said Elizabeth. "We're not denying that it's real *now.* We're just saying its origins are fictional."

"How can something real have fictional origins?"

"You agree that something fictional can have real origins, right?" asked Andre.

"Yes, of course."

"So this is just the same thing, only the opposite."

I shook my head. "That doesn't make sense."

"I know it's a little hard to believe when you first find out," said Elizabeth sympathetically. "I remember I had trouble getting used to it myself in the beginning."

"Look," said Andre. "When you found out the broom could fly, were you surprised?"

"Of course!"

"Before that, did you think flying brooms existed?"

"No, of course not."

"All right. So real objects with fictional origins, that's just another surprise—another thing you didn't think existed, but it does."

"So what are you saying?" I asked. "Is everything in storybooks actually real?"

"No, not everything. Just some things," said Andre.

"Which ones?"

"Lots of things," said Elizabeth. "Most of the things in this room, for example."

I looked up at the shelf spiraling around and around up to the skylight. There were balls and bells and bowls and books, lamps and brushes, telephones, stuffed owls, hats, clocks, jars, sticks, stones, skulls, several complicated little machines, and a whole lot of boxes. I noticed one box labeled *DOORKNOBS* in Dad's distinctive writing.

"What story is that from?" I asked, pointing to an apple. "*Snow White and the Seven Dwarfs*?"

"Where? Did someone leave the Snow White apple in here?" Elizabeth looked around, craning her neck. "Oh, you mean *that*. That's not fictional, it's just left over from my lunch."

"Okay, what about that clock? The big one next to the window, over the boar's head." I pointed.

Elizabeth looked pleased. "Isn't that lovely? We just got it."

"Here," said Andre. "I'll get it down. See if she can guess what it is." He stood on his fold-down chair and reached overhead. He caught the end of the rope ladder and scrambled up, swinging from side to side. With his long, thin arms and legs, he looked like a spider climbing up a clock pendulum. When he reached the clock, I saw it was enormous—taller than Andre. The perspective had made it look way smaller.

He pulled the pulley over to the clock and strapped it on with bungee cords, then scrambled back down.

Elizabeth lowered the clock on the pulley until it was hovering over her desk. "Take a look," she said.

It was an enormous grandfather clock in an ebony case, with a brass face, hands, weights, and pendulum. The wood was as black as a raven, as ominous as a shadow. Reaching out to brush its smooth surface, I felt that familiar coldness penetrating my fingers.

"I'll wind it," said Andre, reaching out to attach the weights.

Elizabeth put a hand on his arm. "No, don't. Then I'll have to listen to that horrible ticking all day. And the chimes! They make my skin crawl."

"That's the point," said Andre, grinning. "Have you figured it out yet, Sukie?"

"No, I give up. What is it?"

"It's a Poe clock—Edgar Allan Poe—from 'The Masque of the Red Death.'"

"The things in Poe stories are *real*?" Talk about skin crawling! Those stories are horrifying. They're full of the worst, most blood-freezing creepiness: people buried alive, instruments of torture, walking corpses.

"We have the world's leading collection of Poe objects here at the repository," said Andre proudly.

"But who decides what fictional objects are going to be real?" I asked. "Because if it were me, I would definitely not choose Poe."

"Oh, I would! One hundred percent! He's my favorite," said Andre. "There's nobody creepier—nobody. Not even H. P. Lovecraft."

"That's a really good question, actually, and nobody knows the answer," said Elizabeth. "I don't think it will ever be solved in our lifetime. But the short answer is, nobody *chooses*, and it's not at all clear why some fictional objects exist in our world and some don't. Does it have to do with the quality of the writing? Its intensity? Its originality? Its popularity? Something else?

Some combination of factors? The field that studies this question is called literary-material philosophy, and it's a topic of great interest in our community. Some of the recent work suggests that copyright might play a role. Are we done with this?"

I nodded, and she hoisted the clock back up on the pulley. Andre reached for the rope ladder, but Elizabeth stopped him. "That's okay, Andre, you don't have to climb up again. I'll put it back later myself." The clock swayed slowly and terrifyingly over our heads. I wished she would let him put it back on the shelf.

I looked at my broom. "So which story do you think this is from?" I asked.

"Like we said, one of the Hawthorne stories—there's lots of Hawthorne brooms," said Andre. "There's Mother Rigby's broom, of course. And a bunch of the townspeople in 'Young Goodman Brown' ride them. It could be Aunt Keziah's broom from *Septimus Felton*. Or it could be from *Fanshawe* or 'Beneath an Umbrella.' Or maybe even *The Scarlet Letter*."

"But probably not those last three," said Elizabeth. "The brooms in those stories are metaphors and similes. I don't think they'd be strong enough to carry you all the way down the coast."

"Wait—*what*? Metaphors and similes can be *real objects*?"

"Occasionally," said Elizabeth. "They're generally pretty weak—much less vivid than actual plot points. But from time to time, one turns up."

"How do you even know all this?"

"Because this is what I *do*," said Elizabeth. "I'm the associate repositorian for acquisitions. Right now my job is acquiring objects of fictional origin for the Special Collections here. Plus, I have a PhD in literature, which helps me figure out where objects might have come from. And where to look for them in the first place."

I must have looked as stunned and confused as I felt, because she added, "Maybe we should start at the beginning. How much do you know about the New-York Circulating Material Repository?"

"Just what you told me," I said. "That it's a private lending library of objects."

"Right," said Elizabeth. "Most people know that we have a large, diverse collection of objects that our members can borrow. What most people *don't* know is that some of our objects have their origins in fiction. And some of those objects have special powers, like your broomstick. Only a select group of people know about our Special Collections—and now you're one of them."

"Welcome to the club! Usually you have to pass a lot of tests before you get to find out," said Andre. "But you actually flew here on a broomstick, so that makes it kind of pointless to try to keep you in the dark."

"Okay. So if all these things are fictional, what about that doorknob I sold you at the flea market?" I asked.

"From a haunted house," said Andre. "We're not sure which one. Probably from a Mary Wilkins Freeman story. There's a bunch of haunted houses in *The Wind in the Rose-bush*. We were hoping *you* could tell *us*."

Elizabeth took down the *DOORKNOBS* box. "Sometimes when we find these fictional objects without a good provenance, we have a hard time narrowing down exactly which story they come from. Can you tell?" She took a doorknob out of the box and handed it to me.

It felt cold and tingly. I handed it back, shaking my head. "I didn't even know they were *from* fiction—how would I know *which* fiction they're from?"

"Yeah," said Andre. "At first we thought you probably knew more than you do, I guess. You must have strong perceptions, though—you can obviously recognize stuff like these doorknobs and that house in New Hampshire you showed us."

"Is that why the doorknob feels so . . . funny?" I asked.

"Probably," said Andre. "Funny how?"

"Sort of . . . cold and tingly."

"Yeah. I guess touch is your special sense. With me it's vision," he said. "Fictional objects of power look kind of shimmery to me."

"With me it's smell," said Elizabeth.

"So you can *smell* when something's fictional? Is that why you're always sniffing things?" That explained a lot, I thought. Though not nearly enough.

Elizabeth nodded. She put the doorknob back in its box and stuck the box back on the shelf. "It's too bad we didn't find the actual house this came from before it got demolished," said Elizabeth. "It would have made a great addition to the Poe Annex."

"The what?"

"My pet project. We're putting together a collection of haunted houses from American fiction. Your dad's helping us with it. Well, so are *you*, actually—you're the one who called us from that Flint house! We've collected over three dozen haunted houses so far."

"Not just houses," Andre put in. "We have gardens, too. And a vineyard and a schoolhouse from Charles W. Chesnutt stories. And a mill and a few castles."

"Wait! You mean that house I found—the one you bought—is *fictional*?"

"Yes," said Elizabeth. "It's from a story by Laetitia Flint, 'The Bobbin Bones.'"

"But I just read that story! The one with the haunted sewing machine, right? Where the bobbin thread keeps breaking, and the heroine has to find the ghost's bones and rebury them or she'll never finish making her wedding dress?"

"Right," said Elizabeth. "At that point in her career, Flint was trying to keep up with her literary contemporaries. You can see the influence of Mary Wilkins Freeman and even a little Edith Wharton in that story, with the focus on domestic details. But it still has Flint's signature sentimental melodrama. I'm surprised you've read it, actually. She's not that popular nowadays."

"Yeah, she's a little over the top, but I like her. My cousin has her complete works in her library. I can't believe it's really that same house!"

"I like Poe better," said Andre.

"Of course you do," said Elizabeth affectionately. "You like Poe better than everything, you bloodthirsty creature."

"Yeah, that's true. Horror beats gothic, no contest. More action, less melancholy."

"Remember that time you talked Leo into helping you

build a model of the pit and the pendulum? And you tried to trap Griffin in it? How old were you, eleven?"

"Ten. And I did not!" Andre protested. "Griffin *volunteered.* I would never try to trap him! Anyway, can you imagine anybody actually trapping Griffin anywhere, no matter how hard they tried?"

"Well, there *was* that one time . . ." Elizabeth looked at me. "Sorry, Sukie. We're being rude, talking about people you don't know. Did you have more questions?"

I did. I had a million questions—too many to ask. An ocean liner full of questions had docked at the wharf of my brain, and they all poured out over the gangplank, wearing funny clothes and carrying bundles. Now they were all yelling at once, and none of them spoke English. I shrugged.

"What about that other thing?" prompted Andre. "Besides the broom. Didn't you say you wanted to show us something else?"

"Right." I found myself strangely reluctant to take out the clasp in this tiny, cramped room, but I made myself do it. "I found this at an estate sale this afternoon," I said, holding out the box. "The second I touched it, I knew it was . . . I don't know, something scary. Something bad. And that guy with the pipe, Adolphus T. Feathertop, he was there too, which seemed weird. Why would he show up all the way up in Rhode Island? He tried hard to buy it from me, but I didn't sell it—even though he offered a lot of money that I could really use. What is it? Should I be worried?"

Elizabeth took the mint tin and opened it. She unwrapped the clasp.

Andre gasped. Both of them stared in silence.

"Yes," said Elizabeth. "Yes, you should be worried."

This was when Kitty decided to put in an appearance.

Kitty materialized on top of Elizabeth's desk. Well, that's not quite the right word—she didn't become solid, just dimly visible.

Andre blinked and frowned, squinting. "Watch out! Something's here," he said. "Don't let it get the Yellow Sign!"

Elizabeth snapped the lid back on the box, sniffing the air. "You're right. I definitely smell something," she said. "Where is it?"

Andre said, "The shimmering's right on your desk."

Kitty wanted to know who these bozos thought they were, *sniffing* at her, and what they thought they were doing with that disgusting clasp and all those dangerous objects all over the walls, and could they actually *see* her? She brightened herself, growing so intensely present she was practically glowing.

"Who's there?" asked Elizabeth tensely.

Andre pointed. "It's a *ghost*!" He sounded both alarmed and gleeful.

"It's okay," I said. "It's just my sister. Kitty, get down from that desk. You're freaking everybody out."

Kitty pointed out that there was really no place else to sit.

"You could stick to the wall like you were doing before."

The wall, Kitty also pointed out, had all those shelves all over it, with things poking out. And anyway, people weren't freaking out about where she was sitting. They were freaking out about seeing a ghost.

I had to admit that was true. Especially when Andre said, "The ghost is your *sister*? Your sister is a *ghost*?"

"Yes. Is that a problem?" I said. "You just said you collected haunted houses! Aren't you used to ghosts?"

"Literary ghosts, yes," said Elizabeth. "But I've never met a ghost of a *real* person! I didn't know they even existed. Was your sister real? I mean, was she a real, live girl who died?"

"Of course she was. What else would she be? She's my sister!"

"You sure *you're* not fictional?" asked Andre.

"How could I be? I'm right here!"

"Could a real girl have a fictional sister?" asked Andre.

"Sure," said Elizabeth. "Her sister could be like an imaginary friend."

"Well, she's not," I said. "You can ask my parents."

Kitty didn't like being talked about as if she weren't there.

I pointed out that we were talking about her precisely as if she *were* there. "We wouldn't have been talking about you at all if you weren't here," I said.

"She can hear you?" asked Andre. "Kitty, can you hear me too?"

"She can hear you fine," I said. "She just doesn't exactly *talk*."

"How do you know what she's saying, then?"

I shrugged. "I just do."

"Kitty, why are you here?" asked Elizabeth. "Is it about the clasp?"

Kitty rolled her eyes.

"No, it's about *me*," I said. "Kitty's always been very protective, even while she was alive." I explained about the family curse, my sickly childhood, Kitty taking care of me, Kitty dying, and the blue whistle. I brought it out to show them.

Elizabeth and Andre examined it respectfully and gave it back to me. "It has that shimmer," said Andre. "Definitely an object of power."

Kitty wanted them to stop wasting time and explain about the clasp. I found I did too, so I asked again.

"Right, the clasp. How long have you had it?" asked Andre.

"Just a few hours. I brought it here right after I bought it."

"And how much contact did you have with it? Have you worn it?"

"No, I've barely even touched it. I touched it once when I found it and once when I put it in that tin."

"Good, you should be all right, then. I'm pretty sure you need to have more contact for it to affect you."

"But what *is* it?" I was getting impatient.

"It's something called the Yellow Sign," said Elizabeth. "It's from a book called *The King in Yellow*, which is a collection of stories about a book called *The King in Yellow*."

"*The King in Yellow* is a book about itself?"

"I'm sorry—I know it's confusing. No, the book the clasp is *from*—by a writer named Robert W. Chambers—has the same title as the book it *discusses*, but they're two different books. The Chambers book is about what happens to people who read the book within the book."

"What *does* happen to them?"

Andre said, "Basically, they all run mad, and some of them die mysteriously."

"Oh." That didn't sound good. "What about the Yellow Clasp, though?"

"The Yellow *Sign*," Elizabeth corrected me. She opened the box and pointed. "See this letter thing? It's the sigil—the sign—of the King in Yellow. In the book, the characters who wear this clasp with the Yellow Sign on it run mad and die mysteriously too."

"Does the clasp drive them crazy and kill them?"

"We think so. Of course, all the ones who wear the clasp also read the book, so it's possible the clasp is harmless on its own."

"It doesn't feel harmless," I said.

"No," she said. "It doesn't smell harmless, either."

"What's *The King in Yellow* about, anyway? The dangerous *King in Yellow*, I mean, the book within the book."

"Nobody knows for sure," said Andre. "Nobody's read it, for obvious reasons. The librarians won't let me borrow it. Not even Libbet. I keep asking."

"We're all rather fond of you," said Elizabeth. "We don't want you to run mad and die mysteriously."

"I bet it would be worth it," said Andre. "The way Chambers describes it, it sounds awesome. All that stuff about twin suns sinking into the lake of Hali, and Carcosa where black stars hang in the heavens, and the shadows of men's thoughts lengthening in the afternoon. And the Pallid Mask. If you let me read it, I bet I could figure out how to get hold of the Pallid Mask!" he said to Elizabeth. "You'd like that, wouldn't you, Dr. Associate Repositorian for Acquisitions?"

"Nope, sorry, no. Nopity nope nope no. Not going to let

you run mad and die mysteriously, not even for the chance to get the Pallid Mask. Your brother would kill me."

He made a face at her, but I could tell he wasn't really mad.

"If this thing is so dangerous, what should I do with it?" I asked, pointing to the clasp with the Yellow Sign. "I don't feel safe keeping it at home. What if somebody finds it and runs mad? Could I—I don't know, donate it to the library here or something?"

Andre's eyes lit up greedily. My sister frowned. She liked the idea of my getting rid of the clasp, but she didn't want me to get cheated since I'd spent all my birthday money on it.

"Are you sure you want to do that? It's pretty valuable," said Elizabeth.

"Would you guys want to buy it, then?"

"We certainly would, but it's worth more than money," said Elizabeth. "What if you leave it here on loan with us, and we can think about a fair price—maybe work out a trade?"

Kitty nodded.

"All right. My sister approves." She had faded to her usual see-through pallor. I wondered if all that brightness tired her out.

Elizabeth got a quill pen and a bottle of ink out of her desk and carefully wrote out a receipt, which I tucked in my pocket.

"What time is it?" I asked.

Elizabeth looked at her watch. "Almost six."

"Yikes! I better get going." I got to my feet and moaned. My arms still ached from my broomstick ride and my legs were chafed in embarrassing places. I didn't see how I could face the ride back.

Andre jumped up too. "You look tired. I can run you home," he offered.

"You mean on the flying carpet?" asked Elizabeth.

They had a flying carpet here?!

"No, that would take too long. I can carry her. I still have the boots checked out."

"Right, sounds good."

"How are you going to carry me home? It's more than two hundred miles!"

"That's okay, they're seven-league boots. I may not be a basketball star, but you don't look that heavy. Where's your house, exactly?"

I told him the Thorne Mansion's coordinates.

"You can call us any time if you need help, Sukie, or if you just have questions," said Elizabeth.

"Thanks. I don't really have a phone, though."

"Oh, right. Hang on." She rummaged around on her desk and handed me a little silver bell. "Ring this when you want to talk, and we'll call you on your phone like we did last time."

"I'll go get the boots. Meet you up on the roof," said Andre.

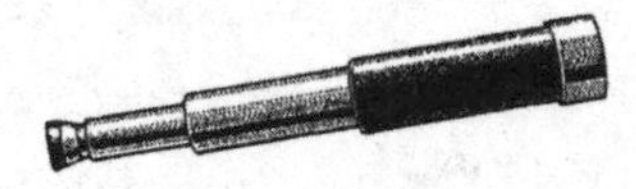

CHAPTER SEVENTEEN

Phineas Toogood's Kiss

"You know how to get to the roof?" asked Elizabeth. I shook my head. "No, of course you don't—this is your first time here, isn't it? Griffin better show you."

She put two fingers in her mouth and let out an earsplitting whistle. A minute later, an enormous nose pushed the door open a crack and an eye peered in. "Griffin, can you take Sukie up to the roof?" Elizabeth leaned around a pile of stuff on her desk and held out her hand to me. "It was good to see you again. Nice to meet your sister, too. Get home safe."

"Thanks for all your help." I zipped up my parka, picked up my broom and backpack, and squeezed through the door.

The gigantic dog set off down the corridor, his nails clicking. He stopped expectantly in front of the elevators, so I pressed the up button. When the elevator came, he gave a little bark. It sounded like "Roof!"

I looked for a button marked *roof* but there wasn't one, so I just pushed the top button. "Is that what you meant?" I asked.

He sniffed.

Kitty thought it was ridiculous of me to have a one-sided conversation with a dog.

The top floor was way fancier than the floor with Elizabeth's chimney office. We passed rooms paneled in oak and mahogany, rooms with mural-painted ceilings, a room lined with card-catalog drawers, and a big room with rows of tables and fantastic stained-glass windows on all four sides. I wanted to stop and stare, but Griffin bounded ahead, making me run a little to keep up.

At the end of a hallway, a ladder hung halfway down the wall, with a trapdoor at the top. Griffin stood on his hind legs, hooked his front paws around the bottom rung, and pulled. The ladder slid down. He bent his head, stuck his nose in the small of my back, and nudged me up.

"Thanks, Griffin," I said, reaching behind me to pet his gigantic floppy ears. Then I tucked the broom under my arm and hauled myself up the ladder.

The sun had set. The roof stood in a grove of tall, twinkly-windowed city buildings, with glimpses of Central Park peeking through. Andre was waiting for me, wearing his hiking boots. They made him even taller.

"So what happens? Do your boots let you fly?"

"No, they're seven-league boots. They make me go seven leagues a step."

"How far's that?"

"About twenty-four miles."

"So, what, you just walk off the roof?"

He nodded. "Don't worry, I've done it before. Lots of times."

“Carrying a person?”

“Carrying a person, carrying a dozen eggs, even carrying a haunted harp one time. Now, *that* was heavy! How do you want to do this—piggyback or fireman’s lift?”

“I don’t know—which way are you less likely to drop me?”

“I’m not going to drop you.”

“I thought you said you were so unathletic?”

“I never said I’m unathletic! I’m just bad at sports. *Big* difference. Fine, fireman’s lift. Ready?” He took me under my arms and swung me around his shoulders, draping me like a scarf. “Comfortable?”

I wiggled a bit to even myself out, feeling very awkward. “More or less.”

“Hang on to that broom,” he said. “That way if you’re worried I’m going to drop you, you can catch yourself.” Then, without bothering to warn me again, he stepped off the roof.

I managed not to scream—I didn’t want to startle him. With my head hanging down and everything blurring together, I started to get motion sickness, so I screwed my eyes shut and hung on tight.

At least it was over fast. “Okay, Sukie!” said Andre eight or nine steps later. “We’re here. I’m gonna put you down now, all right? You can let go.” He shook my arm.

I opened my eyes. He was standing in the field behind my cousin’s mansion, where I’d practiced my flying. He swung me off his shoulders, gently but clumsily. I landed on my butt. He held out a hand and pulled me up, then reached out as if to brush the dirt off my backside. Apparently thinking better of it, he dropped his hand.

"Thanks," I said. "That was quick. So, um . . . do you want to come in for dinner?"

"I'd like to, but my dad's expecting me home."

"Okay. . . . Bye, then."

"Bye!" He waved over his shoulder, took a step, and disappeared.

Flying broomsticks! Magic boots! I wondered how I would travel next. On that magic carpet, maybe? A pirate ship?

I thought about the dim portraits of my ancestors hanging on Cousin Hepzibah's walls—the men in top hats and the ladies in frilly lace caps with their serious faces. They must have flown around on broomsticks themselves. I wished I could have seen it.

Once Kitty and I were alone together, she let me know how furious she was. How could I trust those awful people and their monster dog? They weren't family! They weren't friends! I didn't even *know* them! They were *dangerous*—and they could *see* her! How could I have let that awful giant carry me like a sack for hundreds of miles? How was she supposed to keep me safe if I was going to go running around with people like that?

"Kitty O'Dare, I am not a baby!" I yelled, just as I had yelled a thousand times when I *was* a baby. "I'm older than you are, now! You can't tell me what to do anymore, just because you always did!"

I thought of what Cousin Hepzibah had told me—that ghosts don't change and can't understand when we do. But I couldn't stop myself from ranting. "You know why kids treat me like a freak? Because I *am* a freak—I'm a freak because of *you*! And *I'm* not the one who needs protecting. I'm *perfectly fine*! You're the one who's DEAD!"

Kitty's eyes blazed white lightning. She reared up like a tree in a gale. She was enormous. I'd never been afraid of her before, but now terror seized me. I tried to run, but my feet were rooted to the ground. "Stop it, Kitty! Stop it!" I screamed. A wind tore through the trees, and I couldn't hear my own voice. "Stop it, Kitty! Go away, go away!" I hid my face in my arms.

When I looked up, she was gone. Everything was still and cold and dark. The last time I had felt so alone was the day Kitty died.

It was just as well Andre hadn't come in for dinner. Mom was sitting in the kitchen looking upset, and Dad was comforting her.

A year ago I would have gone away before they saw me, to give them privacy. But now I was older. Hadn't I just told Kitty that? Maybe I could help somehow.

"Mom! What's wrong?"

They both looked up, startled.

"Oh, sweetie, I'm sorry. It's nothing." Mom wiped her eyes.

"It can't be nothing. Can't I help?"

"It's nothing new. Not really. I'm just worried about Cousin Hepzibah. She's pretty strong for ninety-one, but . . ."

I knew what she meant. Mom loved Cousin Hepzibah, but it wasn't just her health she was worried about. "It's us too, isn't it?" I said. If something happened to our cousin, where would we go? "I'll help you, Mom. I can do more." I could sell that jewelry online. I could get Cousin Hepzibah to teach me how to make those lace barrettes and sell them at school. Lola and Amanda had liked them—I bet a lot of the girls would buy them. Or I could sell them online on that craft site.

Who was I kidding? I couldn't support our family selling barrettes.

Dad said, "We'll be okay, Sukie."

Mom said, "You don't need to worry. We'll be fine. We're building up our savings. We've saved a little even just in the time we've been here."

A little would never be enough. I really needed to find that treasure.

I tossed and turned that night, falling at last into a long, muddled dream. I was at the bottom of a pit, which was really a chimney, with a clock ticking far away overhead, its pendulum swinging back and forth, sharp as a blade, getting lower and lower, only it wasn't exactly a pendulum, it was the evil letter from the evil clasp. Darkness began to close in on me, pressing against my skin like dense, wet, choking wool until I felt I was being buried alive. Then the bottom dropped out beneath me. One by one all my arms and legs dropped away separately, as if I'd somehow come apart like a skeleton, and each bone went crashing down, down, down, each bone screaming for all the other bones that were no longer me, just scattered pieces of something that had once been somebody.

I choked on a scream, trying to catch my breath.

Then someone was holding me, rocking me. Andre, I thought, shaking with relief. He had promised not to drop me, and he hadn't. "Hush now, my own one," said a voice, a man.

"Hush now, my Hepzibah. Japhet can't hurt you now. I've got you safe."

I opened my eyes and saw that it wasn't Andre at all, but a familiar-looking stranger. His long, silky black hair was pulled back in a ponytail, revealing sharply contoured cheekbones above a taut jaw. He was looking at me with storm-gray eyes full of anxiety and love. He pulled me closer, then kissed me.

The kiss was like nothing I'd ever imagined. It was cold, colder than the ocean in winter, and stronger and wilder too. The world spun and crashed, broke and foamed around that kiss like waves in a storm. I should have been scared, but I wasn't. The storm was tossing ships to their doom against rocks, sweeping barrels off deck and smashing them, but I wasn't a sinking ship. I wasn't a broken cask. I was the storm itself, wild and exultant—and somewhere deep in the center, cold and still.

Then a bell tolled—a church bell? A bell buoy?—and the kiss ended. He lifted my left hand. "Your ring! You're not wearing your ring! Did you lose it? Did you leave it in the desk drawer again? You must wear it. Promise me you will."

"I promise," I whispered.

"I'll come back to you, Windy," said the man. "I promise too. Nothing will stop me. Not even death." He took my hands in his cold hands and squeezed them. The bell stopped tolling, and he was gone.

I sat up in bed, shivering. What a dream! I rubbed my eyes.

My finger felt empty, the way it does when you've been wearing a ring for a few days and then you take it off. I got out of bed, wincing at the cold floor, and went over to the desk. What drawer? I opened them all in the moonlight, more and more frantically. My ring! I needed my ring! What ring? I thought with part of my mind, but some other part seemed to know. That was the part that found the false bottom in the left-hand drawer and pulled out a little leather box. A silver ring gleamed inside. I slipped it on and sighed.

I was chilled through and too freaked out to stay in my room, so I pulled on my bathrobe and crept downstairs, the bare wood floor cold and creaking under my feet.

Cousin Hepzibah was sitting by the kitchen hearth. She had her lap full of the grandmother pants I'd gotten from the woman at the house sale.

"I couldn't sleep, so I thought I'd see if I could alter these for you. I noticed your own trousers were getting a little short," she said.

"Thank you, Cousin Hepzibah! You're the best."

"Well, I like to sew. It's soothing. Here, hold these up to your waist. Yes, that looks about right. You couldn't sleep either?"

I shook my head. "Crazy dreams."

"Warm milk?" She started to get up.

"Thanks, I can get it." I reached down a mug and poured some milk from the saucepan on the stove. "Want more?"

"Yes, please."

I took her mug and refilled it. As I handed it back to her, she touched the ring.

"This looks antique. May I take a closer look?" she asked. I slipped the ring off my finger. She looked it over and read the inscription inside it: "P.B.T. to H.T.T. Your Heart is my Home."

"Why, that must be Phineas and Windy! It's their initials," she said. "Where did you find it?"

"That's the weird thing. I just knew where it was—in a secret compartment in the desk drawer. Phineas Toogood was in my dream—if it *was* a dream. He . . . he kissed me." I stood still, my fingers to my lips, remembering the kiss.

Cousin Hepzibah shook her head. "Be careful, Sukie," she said. "It's dangerous to get too close to a ghost."

Thinking about Kitty, I knew she was right.

CHAPTER EIGHTEEN

Pirate Toogood's Treasure

I slept late Sunday morning, but I still woke up tired. My parents had driven to the Brooklyn flea market at dawn without me. So much for my offer to do more.

I helped Cousin Hepzibah get dressed and was making my dad's cheesy-chive eggs, still half dreaming about that kiss, when someone knocked on the kitchen door, the one that led to the back porch. It was Cole Farley. For some reason, I was really embarrassed to see him.

"Cole!" I choked. "What's up?"

"Can I come in? I have to talk to you," he said. "It's about that pirate."

"Cole, dear, it's nice to see you," said Cousin Hepzibah.

I went back to the stove. "Want some eggs?"

"Sure—that smells good. Listen, you're never going to believe this! That pirate, Phineas Toogood? He's my ancestor!"

"Come here, child," said Cousin Hepzibah. "Closer." He bent down, and she took his chin in her hand, tilting his head this way and that. "Yes, I can see it," she said at last.

I could too. The cheekbones, the eyes—Cole's were blue,

the dream man's gray, but the shape was the same. The same long black lashes. The same shining hair, if Cole's had been longer and pulled back into a ponytail.

Had it all been just a dream after all? Had I dreamed about kissing *Cole*?

Why would I dream *that*?

I gave the egg pan an angry shake. My ring clinked on the handle. No, not just a dream—dreams don't put real rings on your fingers.

"How do you know?" I asked.

"I was asking my grandfather about pirates. His family's been here for generations, so I thought if he'd heard any stories, that would give us a place to start looking for the treasure. And he told me one of our ancestors was a pirate! Not my great-great-great-whatever-grandfather, but one of his brothers. Grandpa tells great stories about our family, but I never heard that one before."

"How do you know it was Phineas, though?" I spooned the eggs onto three plates.

"That's the part you're not going to believe," Cole said. "Look!" He lifted his right hand. He was wearing a silver ring.

I raised my eyebrows.

He took the ring off and handed it to me. It felt cold, just like mine. "Read the inscription," he said.

I squinted inside the ring. In scrolling letters it said *H.T.T. to P.B.T. Your Heart is my Home.*

"What?! This is incredible! Look!" I handed the ring to Cousin Hepzibah so she could read it.

"Where did you get this?" I asked Cole.

"That's—well, that's the crazy part. I had this dream last night . . ." Was he *blushing*? "About this lady. She looked just like Spooky—like Sukie, I mean—only she was in her twenties, maybe, and wearing these old-fashioned clothes. *Really* old-fashioned, not just grandma pants."

I glanced down at my legs. He wasn't being mean about my new old pants, was he? I thought Cousin Hepzibah had done a great job making them look normal.

Cole went on. "And she told me to wear my ring, and then she . . . well, then I woke up. And I went straight to the fireside cupboard in the old part of the house—our house is really old, like yours, only of course it's way, way smaller than yours—and I found this ring sitting in a bowl. It had to have been there for ages—the bowl was covered in dust. It was like I knew exactly what I was looking for, even though I didn't. I know that sounds crazy. You don't have to believe me."

Cousin Hepzibah nodded. "I believe you," I told Cole. "I mean, it's hard to believe, but I know you're telling the truth." I handed him my own ring. "See? Something similar happened to me."

Cole took the news that we were both descended from ghosts way more calmly than I expected. "I always knew you were special, Spooky," he said. "This just proves it. And of course I always knew I was special myself." He gave that grin of his.

No, the person who freaked out was Kitty—enough to make her appear for the first time since our fight. She hovered beside me, glaring daggers at Cole.

Kitty still saw him as the obnoxious boy who'd teased me

in school. She didn't seem to care that he'd invited me to join his lab group, helped me make friends with Lola, and stuck by me at the risk of alienating his friends. She didn't care that our zillion-greats-aunt had been married to Cole's zillion-greats-uncle, or even that Cousin Hepzibah liked him. Cole Farley was not my friend, Kitty insisted. If I didn't send him away, someone was going to get hurt.

I ducked into the pantry and hissed at Kitty. "Stop it, Kitty! I told you, you need to back off! I'm not a baby anymore, I can take care of myself, and you're wrong about Cole!"

Kitty glared again and vanished with a snap, knocking over a plate.

Her rant made me realize how much I *had* changed my mind about Cole over the past few weeks. Sure, he could sometimes sound obnoxious and full of himself. But everything he actually *did* was pretty decent.

He even washed the cheesy-chive egg plates.

After that, the two of us went up to the library to hunt some more for treasure maps.

"Wow! So this is where you get all those weird old books," said Cole, pulling down a copy of *The Water-Witch* by James Fenimore Cooper and flipping through it. "Have you read this one?"

"No," I said. "But can you help me look through these papers?"

"In a minute. Where are the books you've been reading?"

I pointed to the shelf of Laetitia Flint novels. He pulled one down and began leafing through it.

"Come on, Cole! The map's not going to be in a book."

"It could be. There's a map in this one. Look."

It was Flint's *A Lady's Travels through the Apennines, with Additional Views of the Tuscan Hills.* He was pointing to a map of Italy. "That's not a pirate map," I objected. "It's not even of America. And why would a pirate's treasure map get printed in a book?"

"Maybe it's not printed—maybe somebody stuck it in between the pages. I always hide things in books," he said. "Nobody ever looks there."

"Maybe." I sighed. "This is feeling kind of pointless anyway. I already looked through most of the papers, and I didn't find anything. I doubt it's even here at all. Wouldn't *your* family have it, not mine? Maybe in the old part of your house, where you found Phinny's ring? He died after Windy did, and her family hated him. He could have sent the map back to his own family, couldn't he? If there even *is* a map."

But Cole wasn't listening. "Look at this, Spooky!" he said. "This book—it's about *them*!"

"Them who?"

"Phinny and Windy! Our ancestors!"

"Let me see that!" It was *Flint's Last Works: Being a Collection of Unpublished Stories, Poems, and Meditations by Miss Laetitia Flint, Along with Her Last Novel,* Pirate Toogood's Treasure, *Left Unfinished at Her Death.*

"Look at that last part, *Pirate Toogood's Treasure,*" he said. "It's about *them*!"

"Are you serious? That's incredible! Where? Show me!"

He flipped to it and handed me the book. The novel began in Flint's distinctive overwrought style. "A fierce wind tore at the trim bonnet and tidy skirts of Miss Hepzibah Thorne," I read, "as she leaned precariously against the railing of the lookout atop the Thorne Mansion, a structure termed by our quaint New England ancestors so poetically—and here, so ominously!—a Widow's Walk. She shaded her eyes and peered anxiously at the horizon, seeking in vain the sails of her betrothed: honest Phineas Toogood."

Cole and I stared at each other.

"What are they doing in a *novel*?" said Cole. "I could understand if it was a history book or something, but this is supposed to be *fiction*!"

"I don't know," I said slowly. "But I think I know someone who does."

I rang the little silver bell that Andre had given me. Almost immediately the library phone—the old candlestick style that gangsters use in Prohibition movies—let out a startling trill. I held the cone-shaped earpiece to my ear and spoke into the mouthpiece. "Hello?"

"Sukie? Is that you?" Andre's vowels boomed and his consonants buzzed, but I could understand his words clearly enough.

"Yes, it's me. Wow, you called me back fast!"

"Yes, I'm using the John Murray phone. It's from a ghost story where the dead guy doesn't need a standard telephone connection to make calls."

"Oh, I see. So you're in the repository. Are you with Elizabeth?"

"No, I'm home in Harlem. I borrowed the Murray phone in case you rang. What's up? How've you been?"

Where to begin? "You know the author Laetitia Flint?"

"Sure," Andre said. "She wrote the story that house you found for us is from, remember?"

"Right. Does the repository have any more of her things?"

"Uh-huh, lots. She was one prolific lady."

"Anything from her last novel, the one she didn't finish?"

"That's the one with the pirates, right? I'm pretty sure we've got the pirate's compass. Maybe other stuff too—I can check. Why? You didn't find the house, did you? If you did, Libbet's going to freak!"

"It's not just the house. It's me! I think I'm descended from the characters!"

Andre whistled. "That is *crazy*! Why do you think so?"

"Because I live in the house! The Thorne Mansion!" I told him Cousin Hepzibah's story about Windy and Phinny and how Cole found them in the Flint book. "You believe me, right? I swear, Cousin Hepzibah isn't confusing the family history with the story in the book. She's pretty old, but her memory's fine. And besides, I've seen their ghosts myself. And so has Cole!"

"Are you home? Stay there. We're on our way."

Andre and Elizabeth arrived almost before I had time to explain them to Cole—and definitely before he had time to accept the concept of a library full of haunted houses. "If the houses are from books, how do they get out of the books?" he wanted to know.

"I have no idea. Same way we did, maybe? Apparently we're

from a book too. I know, this sounds totally insane, but I swear, it's true. You'll see when you meet them."

The doorbell sighed its melancholy chime.

"There they are now," I said, hauling the window open and sticking my head out. "Hang on, I'm coming."

Cousin Hepzibah was sitting by her usual window in the drawing room, tatting lace. "Wasn't that the doorbell? Are you expecting guests?" she asked me.

"Yes, I'm about to go let them in. They want to talk to us about the house. I hope that's okay."

"Not more people trying to buy it!" said Cousin Hepzibah. "Do they want to tear it down too?"

"No, if anything they would want to preserve it. I think you'll like them."

"I'm sure I will, if you do. But I'm not selling the house."

"That's all right—they're not here for that. They're here to talk about our history and help us look for the treasure."

"All right," said Cousin Hepzibah. "You can show them in. Just give me a hand, will you, child?" Cole helped her out of her chair while I went to open the door.

Griffin was standing on the doormat. He licked my hand politely and wagged what would have been his tail, if he'd had one.

"Hi, Sukie!" Elizabeth was carrying her walking stick. She looked elegant in riding boots and a tweed skirt and jacket, her hair curling around her face in tendrils as if she'd been riding through mist and wind—which, I reflected, she probably had.

"Is that a Hawthorne stick?" I asked. "That witches ride on?"

"Good guess! Yes, this one's from the short story 'Young Goodman Brown.'"

Andre stepped out of nowhere a second later. He had on the seven-league boots. He kneeled to untie his boots. He was nearly my height that way; if I'd leaned forward, we could have touched noses. He looked up, saw me looking at him, and smiled slowly. "Hi, Sukie," he said.

"Come in and meet Cousin Hepzibah," I said quickly.

Griffin bounded up to Cousin Hepzibah and put his head in her lap as if she were his own long-lost cousin.

"Well, hello there! What big velvet ears you have! Mind if I keep this one? I could use it to reupholster my footstool."

Griffin licked his nose and snorted.

"This is Andre Merritt, and that's Dr. Rew," I said.

"How do you do?" Cousin Hepzibah let go of the ear she was petting and shook hands with each of them.

"Please, call me Elizabeth."

Cole stood up straight and said, "I'm Cole Farley."

"What's up, Cole?" Andre answered. "Is it true? Are you two really Laetitia Flint characters?"

"I don't think so," I said. "At least, we're not in the part I read. Maybe we show up later. I didn't have a chance to finish it yet."

"Huh. Neither did Laetitia Flint," said Andre.

"Actually, Andre, I know you're joking, but you kind of have a point," said Elizabeth. "Flint wrote about the nineteenth-century descendants of the Thornes and the Toogoods. She didn't put any twenty-first-century kids in the book. But she never finished it—maybe if she'd kept going, she would have invented these two."

"Me, maybe," said Cole. "Nobody could invent Spooky."

"Uh, thanks," I said. "Cousin Hepzibah, did you know about this book—Laetitia Flint's unfinished novel, the one with Windy and Phinny in it?"

"Of course, dear. How else would I know about their story?"

Cole and I looked at each other. I could see we were thinking the same thing: Was it all just a mistake, then? Maybe Windy and Phinny weren't our ancestors—maybe they weren't real people at all, just characters Cousin Hepzibah had read about in a book. That made way more sense than being descended from fictional characters.

But then I saw another thought seem to pass behind Cole's eyes, just as it was hitting me too. The ghosts—the ghosts and the rings. I'd seen Phinny, and we'd both seen Windy. We had their rings on our fingers. That had really happened. It was proof.

Then another thought occurred to me. "How do we know Windy and Phinny were fictional?" I asked. "Maybe Laetitia Flint just wrote a story based on real people who happened to be our ancestors."

"Yes, that's the way I always assumed it happened," said Cousin Hepzibah.

"It's a plausible theory," said Elizabeth, "but I can tell you from my years and years of experience with fictional-material houses, we're in one now. This is the real deal. I can smell it. Did Flint invent your ancestors out of whole cloth, or did she base her characters on your real ancestors? I don't think we'll ever know for sure, and I bet the answer is both. Or somewhere in between."

Andre walked over to a window and brushed the glass with his fingertips. "Check it out, Libbet!" he said excitedly. "This window glass is all wavy and green, like Flint describes in the book. It feels real. I bet they're the original panes!"

Elizabeth took a copy of *Flint's Last Works* from her shoulder bag and handed it to him. "Show me," she said.

He thumbed through it and read, "'Looking out the window, Obedience saw her sister as if through a wave of the deep, transfigured by the minute ripples and bubbles of the glass into something rich and strange.'"

"You're right," said Elizabeth. She went to the window and sniffed at the glass, peering through it.

Andre pointed out the window. "And those could be the 'crows that foretell change,' up there on the oak."

As if they had heard him, the three birds squawked in unison and took off from the tree.

Elizabeth turned back from the window. "Your house is astonishing, Ms. Thorne," she said. "I've never seen a better preserved example of literary-material architecture."

Cousin Hepzibah shook her head. "Hardly well preserved. The entire roof needs replacing."

"Even so, the spirit here is as strong as anything I've ever encountered. You've kept it safe. You have a treasure here."

"Thank you. Would you like to see the rest of it?"

"Oh, yes! Could we?"

As Cousin Hepzibah led us all through the ground floor,

Elizabeth and Andre kept stopping to exclaim over details they recognized from Flint's unfinished novel. They identified old Obadiah's easy chair, the little sitting room where Windy turned down Japhet's proposal, and the desk where he opened the cask containing Phinny's hand. Cousin Hepzibah's music room turned bedroom—part of a nineteenth-century addition to the mansion—was where that generation's Hepzibah Thorne played duets with Robert Toogood, a descendant of one of Phinny's brothers. It had a plaster frieze of harps and flutes running around the walls just under the ceiling.

"Robert Toogood must have been my great-great-great-something-grandfather," said Cole.

"I wish I could show you upstairs, but my arthritis is pretty bad today," said Cousin Hepzibah.

"I could carry you," suggested Andre.

"No, let me," said Cole quickly.

"Why don't you do it together?" said Elizabeth.

"Well . . . all right. Thank you," said Cousin Hepzibah.

Cole and Andre made a chair with their arms—Andre had to lean down a little awkwardly to keep it even.

"It's been years since I've been up here," said Cousin Hepzibah when they set her down in the attic. "The leaks look worse than I remembered."

Elizabeth pointed out Beedie's rag doll and a small piano—she called it a spinet—that might have been the one the sisters learned to play on.

Cole and Andre even carried Cousin Hepzibah up to my tower room. I wished I'd made my bed that morning, but at least the bed had curtains. I pulled them hastily shut.

"It's so clean up here now," said Cousin Hepzibah. "Well done, Sukie."

"This was Windy's room, wasn't it?" asked Elizabeth. "In the book, she has the tower room under the widow's walk."

"Yes. It's still her room," I said. "At least, this is where she tends to appear."

Elizabeth's eyes lit up. "Can you call her forth? I would love to meet her!"

I shook my head. "The only ghost I can call forth is my sister."

Cole apparently found that harder to take than the idea that our ancestors were characters in books. "Your *sister* is a ghost? A real, live ghost? I mean a real, dead ghost? Your dead sister?"

I nodded.

"Wow, that explains a lot!" said Cole. "I want to see her. Call her, okay?"

"No, that's not a good idea."

"Why not? Come on, Spooky—a real ghost! I *need* to meet her!"

"No," I said again. "We're not really getting along right now, me and Kitty. She disapproves of the whole treasure hunt—she thinks it's dangerous. And I'm afraid she's not so crazy about you, Cole."

"Me? Why would anybody not like *me*?"

Andre snorted. "Are you ready to go back downstairs, Ms. Thorne?" he asked. "Come on, Cole."

"Thank you again for showing us your amazing house," said Elizabeth, once we were all in the drawing room again.

"It's a pleasure—I'm happy you appreciate it," said Cousin

Hepzibah. "Most people just want to tear it down and build some monstrosity instead."

"Oh, no! You're not considering selling it, are you?"

"Not so far. But I don't know how long we'll be able to afford it. It needs a lot of very expensive repairs."

"That's why we have to find the treasure," I said.

"If you ever do decide to sell, will you call us first?" said Elizabeth. "We would keep your house perfectly intact, ghosts and all."

"How would that work?" asked Cousin Hepzibah.

"We have an annex, where we keep our literary-material structures. If you don't mind a little trip to Manhattan, I can show you."

"I'd like that, but I don't travel so well these days," said Cousin Hepzibah. "Cars don't really agree with me, and I'm far too old for broomsticks."

"Next time, then," said Andre. "We can bring transport. Meanwhile, though, the repository does have Pirate Toogood's compass—I checked. Maybe it'll help us find your treasure."

"That repository sounds awesome! So does a pirate's compass! Let's go *now*!" said Cole.

He looked so eager, I had to laugh. "I'm ready whenever you are. You'll like it, Cole," I said. "It's totally your kind of thing."

CHAPTER NINETEEN

The Lovecraft Corpus

The trip to the repository took longer this time. Elizabeth and Andre flew together on Elizabeth's walking stick, and Cole and I doubled up on my broom. I had to keep slowing down so Cole could get his balance.

"Why aren't you using your boots?" I called to Andre, swooping closer so he could hear.

"They're too fast. Got to stick with you, make sure you don't get lost."

"Can't Elizabeth show us the way?"

"Libbet? Ha. She could get lost in her own bathroom."

As I wobbled upward through a cloud with Cole hugging me a little too tightly around the waist, I was glad I'd practiced flying with my sister. I just hoped I'd practiced enough.

I remembered Kitty teaching me to ride a bike. Kitty standing at the end of our cul-de-sac to keep the cars away, like a redheaded flag post. Screaming at me, "Pedal, Sukie! Harder! *Turn!*" And then, when I finally caught the knack of it and she let me ride my bike after hers out onto the quiet streets of our neighborhood, I'd never felt so proud and alive.

For a wonderful moment a couple of weeks ago, as we looped through the air together, I had felt almost as though I'd never lost her.

But a ghost is not a sister, not really. As Cousin Hepzibah had pointed out, Kitty was stuck in the past, unable to change, while I was growing past her. I was starting to think I couldn't have both Kitty and my real life. Especially not my new friends, Cole and Lola, Elizabeth and Andre. Even Griffin.

"Hey!" I said suddenly. "Where's Griffin? We left him behind! We have to go back!"

"Don't worry, he'll be along soon," said Elizabeth. "He likes to go haring off after eagles, but he always gets where he's going in the end."

Sure enough, the gigantic dog was waiting for us on the roof of the repository when we landed. "Rrrup!" he greeted us.

Cole leapt off the broom and held out his hand to help me down. "That was awesome!" he said.

"Do you believe me now?" I scrambled stiffly off the broom.

Cole said, "It's not that I didn't believe you before. But there's believing and then there's . . . flying."

Cole and I followed Elizabeth and Andre to a room lined with card files.

"Oh, good—there's Dr. Rust, the head librarian," Elizabeth said. "Come on, I'll introduce you."

Dr. Rust looked like a small, friendly middle-aged lion, with a thatch of reddish hair and even more freckles than my sister. "What a treat! You're the first fictional girl I've ever met. At least, that I know of. Cole, are you another fictional cousin?"

"I don't think so—well, I guess I could be. Our ancestors are in the same book. Wow, that sounds so weird." He made a face.

"I'm not sure we're fictional, actually," I said. "Does having fictional ancestors make you fictional yourself?"

"It certainly makes you interesting," said Dr. Rust. "What brings you to the repository?"

"They're looking for buried treasure," Elizabeth said. "From *Pirate Toogood's Treasure*."

"What we really need is a treasure map," said Cole.

"Well, we have several of those—you can look in the subject catalog. We have old Peter's parchment from 'Peter Goldthwaite's Treasure,' and a bunch of Captain Kidd maps, including the one from Poe's 'The Gold-Bug.'"

"What's 'Peter Goldthwaite's Treasure'?" I asked.

"It's a Hawthorne story about a man whose great-great-uncle supposedly sold his soul to the devil for gold and hid the money in his mansion. The map's illegible, so the great-grandnephew ends up tearing down his house looking for the treasure."

An illegible treasure map didn't sound all that useful. "Does he find the treasure?"

"Sort of," said Dr. Rust. "But it's not gold, just worthless bonds and colonial paper currency."

"Sometimes I hate Hawthorne," said Andre.

"I know what you mean," said Elizabeth.

"What about that other parchment, the bug one?" asked Cole. "What's that?"

"You never read 'The Gold-Bug'? It's one of Poe's most famous stories," said Andre.

I made a face. "I find him kind of creepy."

"You say that like it's a bad thing," said Andre.

"Not everyone has your appetite for gore," said Elizabeth. "In 'The Gold-Bug,' a guy finds a solid gold insect next to a piece of parchment with mysterious drawings on it that lead them to Captain Kidd's buried treasure. The parchment's not a map, actually, just coded directions for finding the treasure. What does he call it again, Andre?"

"'A lost record of the place of deposit.'"

Elizabeth went on, "We have plenty of other Captain Kidd material, too. Lots of writers wrote about him. There's that Stowe story, where they use a forked hazel stick like a dowsing rod to look for his treasure. I believe we have the stick."

"Does it work? Or is the Poe parchment legible? Could we use it to find Captain Kidd's actual treasure?" Cole asked. "Is Kidd's treasure real or fictional, anyway?"

I shook my head. "It doesn't matter. We're not Kidd's heirs," I said. "Those maps and parchments and sticks are all for finding other treasures from other books, right? They won't help us. We need Laetitia Flint's."

"Yeah," said Andre. "You're right. They're not really relevant. But they're still pretty cool."

Elizabeth, meanwhile, had been copying numbers from a card in the author catalog onto a slip of paper. She waved the slip. "Here's the call number for Phineas Toogood's compass. It's downstairs in the Lovecraft Corpus, in the basement," she said. "Hey, I just had a thought! Doc, how would you feel about a trade? We could give Sukie the Flint compass in exchange for her Yellow Sign."

Dr. Rust considered. "That sounds more than fair. Okay with you, Sukie?"

"Totally!" I didn't want that creepy Yellow Sign. "What does the compass do?"

Elizabeth's eyes were twinkling. "Haven't you read the book?"

"Not yet—we just found it. I haven't had time."

"It's a haunted compass. It leads Phineas Toogood to Red Tom Tempest's buried treasure."

"You have that *downstairs*?" said Cole. "What are we waiting for? Let's go!"

The basement of the repository was a long white room with fluorescent tube lights that buzzed and flickered. Dr. Rust led us past rows of metal shelves and cabinets, interspersed here and there with metal doors. It all looked very ordinary, but my hands felt cold and I found that my heart was pounding.

"Here we are," said Dr. Rust, stopping in front of a door with **LC Love Corp* stenciled on it in black paint. "Elizabeth, do you have your key?"

Elizabeth fished in the neck of her blouse, pulled out an iron skeleton key on a long silver chain, and turned it in the lock. Then she squared her shoulders and placed her left hand on the center of the door. When she spoke, her voice sounded deep and hollow.

"Noisome sentinels, stand aside! Yours may be to guard, but mine is to enter. Ope now unto me your tenebrous portal!"

The door swung open with a loud, plopping squeal. A cold wind blew our hair back, stinging our eyes and skin. It carried a stench of rot. Beyond, all was shadow.

"Ugh! Somebody needs to clean out the fridge," said Cole.

I said, "What is this place? Do we really have to go in there?"

"Only if you want to find your ancestor's treasure," said Andre. "Welcome to my favorite Special Collection: the Lovecraft Corpus." He stepped across the threshold.

"Come on, Spooky. Here goes nothing!" said Cole. He grabbed my arm and pulled me after him through the door.

We found ourselves in a shadowy room that seemed to be simultaneously closing in on us and dropping away into vast and terrifying chasms. The place felt crowded and chaotic, like the forests you try to run through in those nightmares where you're being chased by wolves. Threads of fog brushed our faces like cobwebs as we pushed past, leaving a sticky residue on our cheeks. The floor underfoot felt springy yet clinging. Every few steps it suddenly sank; I kept having to grab Cole's arm to keep from tumbling into some wet abyss.

But the worst thing was the charnel reek, which stung our lungs like acid. "It's like walking inside someone's intestine," muttered Cole.

"Slow down, Andre! Where are we going?" I called. "I can't see my feet!"

"Oh, sorry. Hang on." I heard a wet click, and then the floor started to glow unsteadily.

It didn't help much. The flickering light was a sick, yellowy green, and it cast confusing shadows upward. I couldn't tell if we were walking past trees or shelves, cliffs or cabinets.

"Are we almost there?" I asked. My voice sounded more panicked than I meant it to.

"What's the matter, the Corpus creeping you out? I was going to give you a tour, but we can just go straight to the compass if you want," said Andre. "Wait, hang on, take a look at this." He handed me something cold and heavy, the size of a bullet.

"What is it?" I peered into my hand, but I couldn't really make out anything.

"Poe's gold-bug."

"Cool!" I squatted down and held it closer to the glowing floor. The insect had six hideous little scratchy legs, feathery antennae, and black markings on its back that made it look like a tiny skull. Griffin leaned down his vast head, snuffled at it, and sneezed.

"Can I see?" asked Cole.

The horrible little legs tickled my palm as I transferred it to his hand. "Ew! Is it *alive*?" I gasped.

"Not exactly," said Dr. Rust. "I wouldn't call anything in this room alive, exactly. Well, except us."

"But it *moved*!"

"The living are not all that move."

I had to admit that was true. I knew it from personal experience.

"What's the gold-bug for, exactly?" Cole asked. "What does it *do*? You said it leads people to treasure—could we use it to find Phineas Toogood's?"

Andre shook his head, making the shadows flicker oddly up his cheekbones. "No, unfortunately. In the story, they just drop the bug through the left eye socket of a skull that's nailed to a tree to find where to dig. They could have used anything—a pebble or a bullet or whatever."

"Oh, too bad." Cole handed him back the gold-bug.

Andre put it away with a rustling noise and moved on a few paces. "Here's your compass, Sukie." He put a cold, round object in my hand.

Something howled not too far off. As its lugubrious echoes fell away, Dr. Rust spoke. "Let's wrap this up, shall we? This place is a bit too fetid even for me."

What with the trip back through the Lovecraft Corpus and the broomstick ride home, it was dinnertime when we returned.

Cole and I stumbled off my broom in the field behind the house and brushed stray twigs off each other, and he walked me to the kitchen door. "That smells good!" he said.

"Mom must be making her pesto lasagna. Want to come in for dinner?"

"Oh, yeah!"

Mom was taking the lasagna out of the oven when I pushed the kitchen door open. "There you are," she said. "I was starting to worry."

"Mom, Dad, this is Cole Farley. He's lab partners with me and Lola in science class. We just came back from the library." Well, that was kind of true, at least. "Can he stay for dinner?"

Mom and Dad exchanged a glance I couldn't interpret, with a hint of a smile and a hint of alarm. "Come on in, Cole!" said Dad heartily. "Grab a plate and sit down."

"Nice to see you again, Cole," said Cousin Hepzibah.

"Oh, do you two know each other?" asked Mom.

"Yeah, Cousin Hepzibah was telling me about your family when I was here before. She has some great stories! Like my grandpa's. And it even turns out we're related, if you go way back to that pirate."

"Pirate? What pirate?" asked Dad. "You never told me about any pirates, Sally!"

"I don't know that story," said Mom. So Cousin Hepzibah told it again, only I noticed she left out a lot, mostly the parts about the dead baby. She probably didn't want to remind my parents to be sad.

After dinner, Cole offered to help with the dishes, but he looked relieved when Dad said, "Looks like it might snow. I'll run you home in the truck before it starts."

As he was putting on his coat, Cole said, "Don't start that lab project without me, Sukie."

"What lab project?"

"You know! The one we were talking about in the library. With the compass."

"Oh, *that* project!" Was he kidding? I had a magical compass that would help me finally find pirate treasure, and Cole wanted me not to use it?! "I don't know, Cole."

"You can't start without me! Promise you won't?"

I nodded reluctantly.

"You have a science project with a compass? I thought you were doing physiology," said Mom.

Cole made a good save. "It's just the Pitch with her extra credit. Ms. Picciotto, I mean, our science teacher. She's always writing these hard problems in the corner of the whiteboard. It takes serious brains to solve them. That's why I need Sukie."

Mom nodded. She'd seen me working on Ms. Picciotto's extra-credit problems.

When Cole and Dad were gone, I piled up the dishes and filled the sink with hot water.

"Cole seems like a nice boy," said Mom.

"I guess." I shrugged.

"He is," said Cousin Hepzibah. "Warmhearted and respectful."

"I'm glad you're making friends," said Mom.

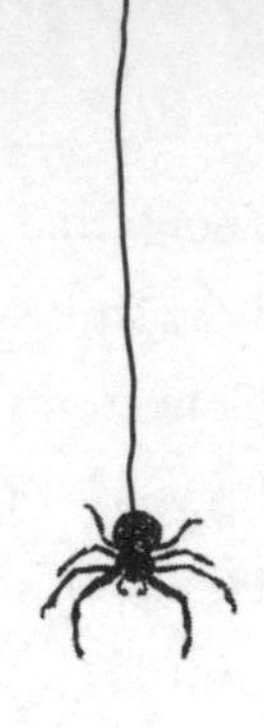

CHAPTER TWENTY

The Poe Annex

Cousin Hepzibah was eager to see the repository annex where they kept the haunted houses, so Elizabeth and Andre arranged to come back to the Thorne Mansion the next Saturday to take us all down.

"Guess what?" said Andre when they called us to discuss the arrangements. "Turns out we have the logbooks from that pirate ship, the *Pretty Polly*! They might say where the pirate buried his treasure."

"Pack your overnight bags if you like," said Elizabeth. "There are plenty of comfortable haunted houses you could stay in, and that'll give us all weekend to search for treasure."

Cousin Hepzibah told my parents she would be visiting friends downstate and had invited me to come along.

"Who are these friends?" asked my mother.

"Librarians. Very kind, scholarly people. I believe you've met one of them, Kevin—Elizabeth Rew. She studies the works of Laetitia Flint, who's a favorite of Sukie's—isn't she, dear?—so they'll have plenty to talk about. She said she would pick us up and bring us home again. We'd like to stay overnight, if that's all right with you. I'll make sure Sukie does her homework."

"Of course, if you want to go, Sukie," said my mother anxiously. She didn't want to offend Cousin Hepzibah, but I could tell she didn't like the idea of me staying with people she didn't know.

"I do want to go," I said. "I love Laetitia Flint, and Dr. Rew is really nice. It sounds awesome."

Dad nodded and said, "Dr. Rew seems nice enough. Have fun, Sukie-Sue. Don't give the librarians too much trouble."

Andre and Elizabeth showed up Saturday morning, timing their arrival for after my parents had left for the city flea markets. Andre was carrying a rolled-up rug across his shoulders, the same way he'd carried me. "Hi, Sukie," he said. "Hi, Cole. Ready to go? I brought a nice, comfortable flying carpet."

Cole pretended to be blasé. "Just let me get Cousin Hepzibah and our bags."

Andre unrolled the carpet on the porch with a flourish, and we piled our backpacks and Cousin Hepzibah's bag on it. Cole climbed on and helped Cousin Hepzibah lower herself to sit down. Elizabeth sat on the carpet too, which lifted off gently, its fringe flapping in the wind. Andre and I flew along beside it, me on my broomstick and him on the Hawthorne walking stick.

We flew between layers of clouds that spangled our hair with silver dew. Cousin Hepzibah had wrapped a large, thin scarf around her broad-brimmed hat, making her look like a passenger in one of those early automobiles.

"Don't worry, it's perfectly safe. It's our steadiest flying carpet," said Elizabeth, but Cole surreptitiously held a fistful of Cousin Hepzibah's coat, just to make sure she didn't slip off.

Dr. Rust met us on the roof and gave us a tour of the New-York Circulating Material Repository. Cousin Hepzibah seemed impressed. "What a well-organized institution," she said. "It's clearly meticulously run. But where is this annex where you hope to keep my home?"

"Down in the basement," said Dr. Rust.

"Where the Lovecraft Corpus is?" I asked with a shudder. "Let's not go in there again!"

"I'm afraid we'll have to," said Dr. Rust. "The Poe Annex is an annex to the Corpus, and the only way in is through the Corpus. But we'll hurry straight through."

"I can get your bag, Ms. Thorne," offered Elizabeth.

"No, Libbet, let me," said Andre, taking the handle from her.

The Lovecraft Corpus was just as abysmal as I remembered, and just as dark. Cousin Hepzibah bore it bravely, leaning on Cole's arm and feeling each step before committing her weight. She did eventually ask, "Are we going much farther, Dr. Rust? I hope you aren't intending to keep my house in *here*."

"No, no," the head repositorian reassured her. "This is where we store our smaller supernatural objects. The Poe Annex is much bigger and more . . . pleasant. We're just passing through here. We're almost there."

Something howled. "We better be," said Elizabeth. "Because that doesn't sound good."

"Don't worry, the gate is just up ahead," said Dr. Rust. "Ah, here we are!"

The gate to the Poe Annex was a tall, vine-twined structure of oak and iron. It creaked when Elizabeth pushed it open. Dr. Rust walked through first and invited each of us visitors in by name: "Enter, Hepzibah. Enter, Cole. Enter, Sukie."

As I passed between the twin granite pillars, I found myself pushing through an icy opposition. It lasted only an instant, then shattered into shards of empty air. I stepped out of the oppressive, reeking, humid gloom of the Lovecraft Corpus into a clean chill.

"Ah! Much better," said Elizabeth.

"Wimp," said Andre. "The Creature was nowhere near us."

"Yeah, well—still. The Corpus is not my favorite Special Collection," said Elizabeth.

We were standing in dim, in-between light—dusk or dawn, I couldn't tell which—at the top of a hill. Stars were fading or just coming out. In the distance I could just make out low mountains, dark forests, groves of towers, the glimmer of water . . . all kinds of different landscapes. The air was crisp and still. I took a deep breath to rinse my lungs.

"Which *is* your favorite collection?" Cole asked. He was still acting blasé, but I could tell he was excited.

"Oh, the Grimm Collection, definitely—with its objects from fairy tales," answered Elizabeth. "But I like the Poe Annex too. We've collected some awesome houses here."

"Why is it so dim?" I asked.

"It's not currently daytime in this exact spot," said Dr. Rust.

"Time doesn't work the same way here—it's not continuous. The annex is crepuscular by default, because lots of items in the collection run to dusk, but there are plenty of pockets of night and day. You'll see. This way."

"Hang on, Doc," said Andre. "Here's something Sukie'll like. You too, Ms. Thorne." He took out a pocketknife, cut two flowers off a bush, and handed one to me and one to Cousin Hepzibah.

It was a rose, white with red streaks on the petals. It glowed dimly in the dusk. "Thanks," I said. "That's beautiful."

"What is it?" asked Cole.

"A Laetitia Flint rose," said Elizabeth. "From her story 'A Bed of Roses,' about a pair of dead lovers. It's variegated because it grows out of their tomb. Red for him, white for her."

"That rose is okay, but be careful of the plants around here," said Dr. Rust. "Don't pick them without asking first. Lots of them are poisonous—or worse."

"Let's head over to the library now," said Andre. "That's where we keep the logbooks from the *Pretty Polly.*"

"You mean we're going back upstairs to the repository? Then why did we come down here?" I asked, confused.

"No, no," said Elizabeth. "We're still *in* the repository, just more *deeply* in it. I'm talking about the Spectral Library—the Library of Fictional Volumes. We'll take the train."

"The train goes through the annex, so Ms. Thorne can see our holdings," said Dr. Rust. "This way."

Holding the Flint rose to my nose, I followed the repositorians downhill. The flower sparked a memory. It smelled like a rose, but not just any rose. It had a spice of carnation or clove under its citrony sweetness.

"Cousin Hepzibah, does that rose smell familiar to you?"

She took a deep sniff. "I think so. It's very much like the one that grows on Windy's grave. Where Phinny's hand is buried."

I knew it then: It was the smell of Windy's ghost.

It was a haunting smell, and it made me sad. I wanted to find that treasure—of course I did. But this was about more than just treasure. When we found it, would it help that lonely ghost find rest?

CHAPTER TWENTY-ONE

The Train Through the Annex

A big, slightly transparent white stone building stretched out in front of us. "This is Lost Penn Station," said Dr. Rust.

"It's huge! What story is it from?" asked Cole.

"It isn't actually fictional, exactly," said Andre. "It was a real train station that got torn down. But everybody loved it so much that it entered into the shared mythology."

"If it isn't fictional, why is it here?" I asked.

"In some real sense, it isn't," said Dr. Rust. "Only its echo is here."

"We have plans to start a collection of Lost Places," said Elizabeth. "That's going to be my next project, after the Poe Annex. All we have so far are a few spots in Manhattan, including Lost Penn Station. We're using it as a train depot until we can acquire a good fictional one."

Inside the station, light streamed down from arched windows a long way up. A woman ran through me, furling her umbrella. Its raindrops spun through the air without wetting me.

"That's not a ghost, is it?" I said.

Elizabeth shook her head. "More like a memory."

"If the people can just walk through us and the building's not really there, why don't our feet fall through the floor?" Cousin Hepzibah asked.

"You're right, they should," said Dr. Rust. "But that would be very inconvenient, so we substantiated the floors. Don't jump too hard."

"The train's this way," said Andre.

We followed him through the vast station, with its lacy ironwork, to the staircases that led to the trains. They seemed much more solid.

"Are these real trains?" I asked.

"Yes—well, fictional trains," said Elizabeth. She pointed to a freight train with an evil look to it. "For example, that one's from a Willa Cather story. It goes way out West. We're taking the train from the Hawthorne story 'The Celestial Railroad.'"

Sure enough, the compass pointed to a platform where an iron monster was belching steam and coal smoke. "All aboard!" said Andre, hopping up on a car, pulling the door open, and ducking his head to keep from hitting it on the door frame. He reached his long arm down to give me a hand up. Cole helped Cousin Hepzibah up next, and Elizabeth scrambled up after us. Dr. Rust shut the door, and the shaking metal monster clattered into motion.

As we rattled through the landscape, Elizabeth and Andre pointed out haunted houses.

"Here's Lyng," said Elizabeth. "Isn't it beautiful?" We

were passing a manor house on a hill, the kind you might see on a TV show about an aristocratic English family and their servants.

"What's its story?" I asked.

"It's from 'Afterward,' by Edith Wharton. An American man makes a lot of money, not very honestly, and buys an estate in England. But the guy he cheated killed himself and starts haunting him."

"Spoiler alert!" said Andre.

"Oh, sorry."

The house disappeared around a bend. "If it's an English house, what's it doing *here*? Are we somehow in England now?" asked Cousin Hepzibah. "It doesn't feel as though we've traveled anything like far enough. Shouldn't we still be in New York, or at most New Jersey?"

"No, we're still in the Poe Annex. Standard geography doesn't apply," said Dr. Rust.

Elizabeth elaborated. "Parts of the Poe Annex do have a relationship to New Jersey, of course. The Annex relates to the New England states, plus a few in the South and the West, and some more distant regions. But there's no one-to-one correspondence with the geography you're accustomed to. You can think of this as a separate dimension from our usual world."

"The geography here in the Poe Annex isn't particularly linear," said Dr. Rust. "We file the items by their call numbers, not continents. Even though 'Afterward' is set in England, it's an American classic—Wharton was an American, and so are the characters and themes."

"Wow, Sukie! Can you believe all this?" said Cole. "I'm totally going to start paying more attention in Language Arts class."

I laughed. "Science, and now Language Arts? Who knew I would turn out to be such a good influence?"

"I did," said Cole. "It was obvious from the way you stuck your nose in a book and ignored me."

We passed a few more fancy English country estates and some gloomy houses, which Elizabeth said were from the ghost stories of Henry James. Cousin Hepzibah looked impressed.

Then the train went through a town with a big house with lots of peaks and gables. "One, two, three, four . . . five . . . Is that the House of the Seven Gables, from the Hawthorne novel?" I asked.

"No, but good guess," said Elizabeth. "It's from a different Hawthorne story, 'Peter Goldthwaite's Treasure'—I think I mentioned it before. The Hawthorne houses all have a certain family resemblance. It's like the way houses designed by the same architect tend to look like each other."

"Hey, it looks a lot like your house, Spooky!" said Cole.

"You're right, Cole. Especially those gables," said Cousin Hepzibah.

"Makes sense," said Andre. "Laetitia Flint was influenced by Hawthorne."

"What about that clump of houses up ahead?" I asked. They looked kind of like the Hawthorne ones, only more modest.

"Those are from Mary Wilkins Freeman stories—she was another writer who influenced Flint," said Elizabeth.

"Remember those doorknobs you sold us? We think they came from one of her stories."

Cole spun around to watch them disappear as we passed. "That last one looks like my house, a little bit," he said. "Do you think mine could be haunted too?"

"Oh, I hope so!" I said. "Then *you* would be the spooky one! What should I call you? Fearsome Farley? Uncanny Cole?"

"Fantastic Farley, obviously. Or—" He put on a deep voice and intoned, *"Cryptic Cole—he's always a surprise!"*

"Here comes one of our coolest houses," said Andre. "Up to the right, see? The Cap'n Brown House. It's from a Harriet Beecher Stowe story and it's haunted by a herd of headless black colts."

"Harriet Beecher Stowe, the author of *Uncle Tom's Cabin*?" I asked. "We read about that book when we were studying the Civil War. I didn't know she wrote ghost stories too."

"Sure, lots of writers did back then. Look left now, we're passing another one of my favorites."

A little wooden structure flashed by. "What was that?" Cole asked.

"The haunted schoolhouse from Charles W. Chesnutt's story 'Po' Sandy.' A man gets turned into a tree, and they make the wood into a schoolhouse. So of course the man haunts it."

"I would too," Cole agreed, "if somebody built a school out of me."

I thought about the many reasons ghosts had for haunting people and places. They wanted revenge, or acknowledgment, or something they lost. Or they were trying to keep a promise from when they were alive, like my sister. It must be so sad to be a ghost and not be able to do anything really new—if you needed something done, all you could do was try to get someone living to do it for you. And half the time the living people couldn't even hear you.

"Here comes the jewel of our collection," said Elizabeth. "We named the annex in its honor."

The train labored toward a medieval-looking stone building with a still lake in front of it. Its unruffled luster reflected the castle's bleak walls and empty, eyelike windows.

"Ooo, creepy," said Cole.

"That's the House of Usher," said Andre proudly. "From the Poe story."

I stared at the house. "Didn't you say we were related to some Ushers?" I asked Cousin Hepzibah.

"Yes," she answered. "I wonder if it's the same family."

"That place looks so dismal," I said. What a gloomy family I'd been born into, so full of ghosts and death! At least the Flint stories sometimes had happy endings—though not for everyone. Just for the hero and the heroine, usually. I hoped I was the heroine here.

"Wait a sec," said Cole. "I read that story. It's called 'The Fall of the House of Usher.' The *fall* of the house. The house *falls down* in the end. It gets completely destroyed. So how can it be here *now*?"

"Thanks for noticing! We're very proud of that," said Elizabeth. "A former page of ours at the repository, Leo Novikov, is doing some really innovative work in fictitious technology. He invented a machine that can select any temporal state in the narrative span of a fictional object."

"I'm afraid I don't quite follow," said Cousin Hepzibah.

Dr. Rust clarified. "If you have an object from a work of fiction, Leo's machine can return it to the state it was in at any point in the story. It's been incredibly useful."

The train dived into a dark wood, then chugged up a hill. When it reached the top, I could see seawater sparkling in the distance. "Almost there," said Andre.

As if the hands of a ghostly brakeman had pulled a spectral lever, the train screeched and rolled slowly to a halt. We shouldered our backpacks, and Cole picked up Cousin Hepzibah's bag. Andre pulled the door open, ducked through it, jumped down, and held out his hand to me. He caught me as I stumbled on the steep step. "Here we are," he said.

CHAPTER TWENTY-TWO

The Spectral Library

Here turned out to be a quaint New England port town with little square white houses and redbrick sidewalks.

"Are we still in the Poe Annex?" I asked.

"Yes, the annex comprises this whole landmass, down to the water. Once you get out on the ocean, though, you're in neutral territory. This is the town of Library Point, from 'The Spectral Librarian,' a short story by Flint. And there's the Spectral Library itself," said Elizabeth, pointing. "The Library of Fictional Volumes."

Ahead of us, silhouetted against a brilliant orange sunset, was a tall, rectangular stone building with banks and banks of windows.

"Fictional volumes?" echoed Cole. "You mean novels and short stories? But why would they keep the ship's logbooks there? Aren't logbooks nonfiction?"

Andre said, "It's not a fiction library. It's a fictional library of fictional books. Some are fictional fiction and some are fictional nonfiction."

"Isn't *all* fiction fictional? Isn't that what the word *means*?"

Cole objected. "And what's fictional nonfiction? That doesn't mean *anything*."

Dr. Rust explained, "The Spectral Library is where we keep books that only exist in books. Like . . . What's a good example, someone?"

"*The Mad Trist of Sir Launcelot Canning*," suggested Andre.

"Exactly! *The Mad Trist of Sir Launcelot Canning* is a work of fiction—it's a medieval romance. But it only exists in the Poe story 'The Fall of the House of Usher.' The narrator reads *The Mad Trist* to his crazy friend. You can't find it in any ordinary library, but we have a copy here in our library of fictional books. It's fictional fiction."

"Okay, what's fictional *non*fiction, then?" I asked.

"Same idea. Not all the fictional books are fiction," explained Dr. Rust. "Some are nonfiction."

"Huh?" Now I was thoroughly confused.

"Oh, for example . . ." Dr. Rust hesitated.

Elizabeth suggested, "*The Key to All Mythologies*?"

"Yes! Good one. That's in *Middlemarch*, a novel by George Eliot. A fussy scholar spends his life writing it—*The Key to All Mythologies*, I mean. It's nonfiction, but it exists in the novel, which is fiction. So it's fictional nonfiction. See?"

"Okay," said Cole, "then why did Andre just call the library a *fictional* library of fictional volumes?"

"For the same reason the rest of our collection in the Poe Annex is fictional," said Dr. Rust. "The library comes from a work of fiction. In this case, 'The Spectral Librarian'—another Laetitia Flint story . . ."

"Actually," Elizabeth interrupted, "if you want to get really technical, you could call it a fictional fictional library of fictional fiction and fictional nonfiction. Because in the Flint story, the narrator finds a manuscript in an old library. The manuscript is called *The Spectral Librarian*, and it's a novel about a ghost librarian who tends the Spectral Library of Fictional Volumes. It's a story within a story. So in the Flint fiction, the library is fictional, which makes it doubly fictional here."

Before my brain could explode, we arrived at the building, which seemed solid enough. Dr. Rust pulled open the doors.

I often dream of libraries, but this was better than all my dreams. It had galleries of books with dimly gleaming bindings. Wheeled ladders leaned against tiers of shelves and filigreed staircases twirled up to balconies, with catwalks spiderwebbing from section to section. Oak tables stretched out under skylights and cozy chairs were nestled beside crackling fires. I wanted to pluck a book from a shelf, curl up in a chair, and stay there forever.

Cousin Hepzibah evidently had the same thought. "Oh, poetry! Here's Christabel LaMotte's *A Selection of Narrative and Lyric Poems*! And Herbert Keanes's *Flowers and Fruit*! And I've always wondered what John Shade's other poems were like." She gathered an armful of books from the shelves and sank into one of the sofas with a sigh of pleasure. Griffin sank down at her feet and put his nose in her lap.

Cole got down to business. "Where are the logbooks?"

"I'm not perfectly sure," said Dr. Rust. "The cataloguing system here is idiosyncratic. We'll need to consult the Spectral Librarian."

"Where do we find him? Or her," I asked.

"There's a bell he answers. This way."

"I think I'll wait for you here," Cousin Hepzibah said. "Enjoy yourselves!"

It was hard to keep following Dr. Rust—I kept wanting to stop and read—and apparently Andre did too.

"Ravisius Textor's *Absurdities*," he said. "That's from 'The Assignation,' by Poe." He flipped pages. "There's supposed to be a list in here of people who died laughing."

"Come on, Andre," said Cole. "We'll never find the treasure if you keep stopping to read."

Andre put the book back reluctantly.

I trailed my finger along the spines of some mysteries. "Which are better," I asked, "real books or fictional books?"

"What an interesting question!" said Dr. Rust. "What do you think, Elizabeth? You've read way more of these than I have."

"It depends. There are lots of terrible imaginary books." Elizabeth waved her hand at the ones we were passing, which had lurid spines. "Bad writers will always produce bad books, even fictional ones. But fictional books can be screamingly funny, especially when a comic genius made them up as satire. Like the *Millie* books, from Diana Wynne Jones's Chrestomanci series. They're so exquisitely terrible, they make me laugh till the tears run down my face. And fictional books have the advantage of staying closer to the writer's conception. You know how sometimes, when you're trying to write something, you start out with a huge, magical, unformed vision, but no matter how well you write the book, it never comes out how you imagined?"

Cole shook his head. "I don't write much," he said.

"Okay, it doesn't have to be writing," said Elizabeth. "Anything that takes imagination—a picture, a song, whatever. Swinging a baseball bat."

I thought about carving pumpkins with Kitty when I was little. My pumpkin never came out anything like the scary ones I saw in my head before I started. Kitty's were always a lot better than mine; the year I was five, I had to use the back door the whole week of Halloween because I was too scared to walk past Kitty's pumpkin on the front porch. It was that good.

Of course, maybe the one in her head was even scarier.

"Fictional books perfectly embody the original conception, so the magic doesn't leak out in the writing process. Here we are, the Reference Room," said Elizabeth.

There was a round brass bell on the corner of a long wooden counter. Dr. Rust walked over and struck it.

The sound of the bell went on and on. It was sweet but dark, like the smell of graveyard roses. Out of the corner of my eye, I saw what I thought must have been the Spectral Librarian standing at the opposite end of the room. He was tall, gaunt, and dressed in something black and flowing—a long coat, maybe, or a scholar's robe.

I turned my head for a better look, but that end of the room was empty.

Confused, I glanced away, and the Spectral Librarian was back.

"Good afternoon, sir," said Elizabeth. (I wasn't sure why she'd decided it was afternoon just now—the sun had been setting last time we saw it.) "Can we trouble you to help us find the logbooks from the ship *Pretty Polly*, out of *Tom Tempest's Treasure*?"

With a sidelong glance, I saw the Spectral Librarian bow and glide toward the center of the wall. A shadow opened in the wall and he wafted through it.

"Come on, Spooky," said Cole, grabbing my arm. We all followed the ghost into the shadow.

It was a confusing trip. Books and shelves and stairs and walls spun past the corners of my eyes, but whenever I tried to look at them directly, they glimmered away like those dim stars you can only see with the edges of your vision. Underfoot I heard my shoes click on stone, creak on wood, or crunch on gravel, but when I concentrated on the sound, it spun into silence, like the silence in a strange house deep in the country at night. So I fixed my eyes on the back of Elizabeth's head in front of me.

Elizabeth had a plastic tortoiseshell clip in her hair. It looked very ordinary. I found that comforting.

"Why the cloak-and-dagger stuff?" asked Cole behind me. "Wouldn't it be easier to just use the Dewey decimal system like everybody else?"

"Cole!" I hissed, worried he was going to offend the Spectral Librarian. But the vague figure kept gliding through the nebulous passage as if it hadn't heard.

"All the best libraries of fictional books have spectral caretakers," said Dr. Rust. "It's a sensible tradition. Safer this way."

"But why?" Cole asked again.

"Well, it obviously doesn't much matter who reads *Millie of Lowood House*. But some of the books here are dangerous."

"Like what?" asked Cole.

Elizabeth said, "Tons. *The Spectral Librarian* itself—you don't want someone messing with the source book while you're inside a fictional structure. *The King in Yellow.* The *Necronomicon.* Most manuals of magic. *The Garden of Forking Paths. The Magician's Book.*"

"I remember that one!" I said. "It's in the Narnia series. One of the characters reads a dangerous spell and gets into trouble."

The hair clip bobbed as Elizabeth nodded. "Books like that need a guardian."

The Spectral Librarian stopped gliding, and I found myself in a compact room with tables bolted to the floor, cabinets running neatly up to the ceiling, and sun streaming through a row of portholes. Outside, light danced on waves out to the horizon. In the corner of my vision, the Spectral Librarian bowed and vanished. I felt a little unsteady, as if the room were gently rocking.

I turned around. On the round table in the center of the room lay a neat stack of leather-bound books that smelled of the sea.

We each took a volume of the ship's log to hunt for clues to the treasure. They were enormous, sharp-cornered volumes that poked you in the lap and kept flipping themselves shut. Only Andre had long enough arms to hold them comfortably.

I wrestled mine to the window seat and laid it open on the hard leather cushion. Phineas Toogood had written with a quill pen dipped in liquid ink by the light of a whale-oil lamp in a cabin that probably rocked like an amusement-park ride. And back then, even tough-guy pirates wrote with loops and flourishes. It took me a while to get the hang of telling the *T*'s from the *C*'s and the *f*'s from the *s*'s.

It was wild to think that Phineas had actually touched these books! Handsome Phineas, with the yearning eyes and the cold, ghostly hands, back when his hands were warm because he was still alive. I turned the pages carefully, imagining him turning them himself. They were stiff and crinkly, like the pages of a book you leave out in the rain and then dry in the sun.

Most of the entries were just brief notes: weather, distance, location, amount of remaining rum. But now and then Phinny would take a quarter of a page to tell a story, like when the ship stopped on a deserted island to take on water, and they discovered three families living in a vast, ruined temple.

"Listen to this, Libbet!" said Andre. "'*The day began with pleasant Weather and a moderate Breeze. Wind freshened at 3 p.m. and sails adjusted. Raised a ship to the Eastern Board, which prov'd to be the* Dolphin *out of Lynhaven. Dined aboard with Cap't Heidegger, the notorious Red Rover. Plum duff excellent.*' Is that the same *Dolphin* here in our collection?"

"Must be," said Elizabeth. "Ours is out of *The Red Rover*, by James Fenimore Cooper. The details match."

"The *Dolphin*'s from a *novel*? What's Laetitia Flint doing with a ship from some other book in *her* book?" I asked.

"She read a lot of Cooper novels, and this one's a rip-roaring pirate story—it must have influenced her," said Elizabeth.

"That sounds like more than just influence." Our English

teacher had given us a strict lecture about plagiarism. Using someone else's ship in your own book might qualify.

"The *Dolphin*'s not in her *novel*, just in her fictional logbooks," Dr. Rust pointed out. "I don't think that really counts, since fictional logbooks aren't exactly published. But objects often cross from writer to writer, through influence. That's probably why you have that Hawthorne broom in your family, for example."

We went back to our books, and the room fell silent except for the swish of turning pages. Then Cole shouted, "Got it! This is it! It has to be!"

"What?" asked Elizabeth.

"'*Sighted Land just after the first dogwatch, which proved indeed to be Broken Isle. Dropped anchor in Northern Cove*'—then a bunch of numbers—that must be the depth or something. Blah, blah, blah, more numbers . . . okay, here. '*We followed the Compass north to a ridge beneath the high hill, where we determined to secrete our Treasure beside that of Red Tom Tempest.*'"

"Let me see that," said Andre. "You're right! Looks like you found it!"

"How do we get there, though? The coordinates are all messed up," said Cole.

We all peered at the book. That volume was even harder to read than mine—apparently it had gotten soaked in a storm or something and the ink had run. The columns for longitude and latitude were completely illegible. "Oh, no!" I moaned.

"Don't worry," said Andre. "We don't need coordinates. Sukie's got something better."

Everybody turned and looked at me expectantly.

"I do?"

"Of course you do! Phinny's compass!"

When I told it to find Broken Isle, the compass went hot, the needle spinning madly. At last it bobbed to a stop, pointing at the door we'd come in by. "I think it wants us to go out."

We all piled our logbooks back on the table, and Dr. Rust thanked the Spectral Librarian. He didn't seem to be around, but maybe he could hear us anyway. My sister often could, even when she wasn't exactly there.

Where *was* Kitty? I wondered. I'd barely seen her since we'd had that fight, the biggest one of our lives. Not just our lives, in fact—our whole time together, living and dead. Still, it wasn't like Kitty to leave me all alone, especially on such a potentially dangerous adventure. Maybe there was something about this place keeping her out? I remembered how Dr. Rust had ushered us into the Poe Annex by name. Maybe she couldn't pass through the portal uninvited?

As uneasy as I'd been feeling around Kitty these days, I felt uneasy without her, too. This was the first time in as long as I could remember that I couldn't feel her looking out for me. What if I got into trouble—what if I needed her? Would she be able to come if I blew the whistle?

I hoped I wouldn't have to find out.

The four others trooped after me as I followed the compass needle down unfamiliar corridors hung with portraits and plaques and through rooms full of books and maps. Unlike an ordinary compass, which always points north even if there's a wall in the way, this one seemed to know not just the right general direction, but the best route to the exit.

"Where *is* this Broken Isle, actually?" asked Andre.

"What do you mean? You saw the logbook—we don't know. The writing was all messed up," said Cole.

"Big-picture where, I mean. What part of the world?"

"Oh. The West Indies. That's where they were sailing in that part of the logbook," said Cole.

"The Caribbean. Too bad. That means I can't use the seven-league boots—you have to touch the ground every seven leagues, so they're no good over open sea," said Andre.

"Broomsticks?" Cole suggested.

"It's kind of far for that, but maybe," Andre said.

"I left mine upstairs in Elizabeth's office," I said. "But if we're going to go flying off over the sea, maybe we'd better take Cousin Hepzibah home first."

"I don't think the compass wants to go back to the upstairs world," Dr. Rust said. "It's taking us out the back way, toward the sea, not to the train."

"The sea is neutral territory," said Elizabeth, "and we don't have any fictional islands. So this Broken Isle isn't in the Poe Annex."

"But, Libbet, then why's the compass pointing— Oh." Andre stopped suddenly.

"Are you thinking what I'm thinking?" asked Elizabeth.

"Jonathan Rigby," said Andre. "I bet it's one of his islands."

Elizabeth nodded slowly.

"Who's Jonathan Rigby?" I asked.

"You remember that guy we keep running up against, the one who smokes a pipe?" said Elizabeth.

"Of course. Is that Jonathan Rigby? I thought he was called something else."

"He is—that's Feathertop. Jonathan Rigby's his boss. Jonathan's a private collector, and his collections adjoin ours in this collection space."

"You met him at the flea market that time," said Andre.

"Oh, yeah, that guy. He really wanted to buy the Hawthorne broom," I said.

"Yeah, he's not a bad guy, but he can get aggressive about his collection. That must be where the compass wants us to go—his collection. Jonathan's not going to be pleased if we start digging on his island, though," said Elizabeth.

"Does he have to know?" asked Cole.

"Well, he's likely to find out. And then there's the issue of who has title to the treasure."

"The treasure belongs to Spooky and Cousin Hepzibah," said Cole. "Obviously! Windy's their ancestor."

"Or to your family," I said. "Phinny's yours."

"We can split it," said Cole, proving once again that Kitty was wrong about him being a jerk. Jerks don't offer to split pirate treasure.

"Rigby's definitely going to claim it if we find it on his island," said Elizabeth.

"Cross that bridge later. Let's find it first," said Andre. He pushed open the library doors.

"I'm going to leave you guys here, okay? I tend to get seasick," said Dr. Rust. "Good luck! I hope you find it."

CHAPTER TWENTY-THREE

The *Ariel* at Sea

We followed the sloping cobblestone streets down to the waterfront, where waves lapped against weathered wooden piers, rocking dinghies and sailboats and making little chuckling noises. Farther out, a forest of larger vessels rode at anchor, scribbling on the sky with their masts.

"Now what?" asked Cole.

"I think the compass wants us to find a boat," I said. "Are any of these yours?"

"All of them," said Andre. "Can y'all sail?"

"Not me," I said.

"I can," said Cole.

"Are we taking one of Phineas's ships?" I asked. "The *Pretty Polly* or the *Sandpiper*?"

"No," said Elizabeth, "they're both too big for the four of us to handle."

"How about the *Ariel*?" suggested Andre. "Out of *The Narrative of Arthur Gordon Pym of Nantucket*."

Elizabeth shook her head at him, smiling. "You do love those Poe objects, don't you? In the book, the *Ariel* sinks."

"In a storm—after a big ship runs them down! And the captain's drunk. The weather looks good right now, and you're not drunk, are you, Libbet? Anyway, the *Ariel*'s the right size. Can you think of anything better?"

"No, I guess you're right. The *Ariel* it is."

We walked along the uneven brick sidewalk to a gray pier that had barnacles growing up its log legs like ragged white socks. A smallish sailboat with a single mast strained against its rope. Andre pulled it closer and Elizabeth jumped on. "Come aboard, you two," she said.

The three of them flew into a frenzy of activity: pulling on some ropes, letting others go slack, raising sails, rocking and tilting, and a whole lot of Andre yelling, "Starboard, Elizabeth! No, *starboard*! That's *port*!"

I kept my head down and tried to keep my feet away from the various ropes whipping around the deck. Soon enough we were skimming out to sea under puffy white clouds, the town blurring to a redbrick smudge behind us.

Sailing, I discovered, is a strangely peaceful way of going fast. On a sailboat, the wind is pushing you forward, which means it doesn't actually feel windy the way it does on, say, a flying carpet or a bike. On a bike, you're moving forward against air that whips your hair back. On a sailboat, you're going *with* the wind. Your hair sometimes even stays put. When you're out of sight of the land and there aren't any other ships around, just the wide, empty ocean, you feel as if you're standing still. You only find out how fast you're really going when you accidentally drop your left mitten over the side and see it zoom away behind you, like a tiny drowning elf.

"Too bad about your mitten," said Elizabeth.

"I wonder if Cousin Hepzibah has any of that red yarn left. Maybe she could knit me a new one."

Of course, every so often one of your traveling companions will shout, "Coming about!" and the second companion—the one at the tiller—will answer, "Hard alee!" and the third will yank you down flat on your face and throw himself on top of you as the heavy wooden beam at the bottom of the sail sweeps across the deck. That part isn't quite so peaceful.

And then there are the squalls. Those aren't peaceful, either. The sky goes green-yellow-gray, the wind whips around and hurls stinging water up your nose, and your shipmates yell at you to haul on various lines, or at least get out from underfoot, you errant lubber!

Okay, so maybe sailing *isn't* such a peaceful way to travel fast.

After one of the squalls, the sun came out and twinkled on a sail. "Ship ahoy!" said Cole. Andre ducked downstairs into the main cabin and came back with a trumpet-shaped object and spyglass, which he held to his eye.

"Who is it?" asked Elizabeth.

"Hm . . . three masts, a tiller . . . lots of bone—got to be a whaler . . ."

All this time, the ship had been drawing closer. A figure came on deck, held its own trumpet to its mouth, and yelled. The words rolled clearly over the now-still water: "Hast seen the white whale?"

"Oh, it's the *Pequod*!" exclaimed Elizabeth. She took the trumpet and yelled, "Very funny, Rachel. Ha, ha, ha."

"Rachel can't hear you," said Andre. "Wind's coming toward us."

"You're right. Is it worth getting out the signal flags?" Elizabeth made big beckoning gestures with her arms at the other ship.

"Who is that?" Cole asked.

"My husband's cousin. She collects fictional Americana. That's her prized possession—the whaler from *Moby-Dick*."

The two women lowered their speaking tubes and waited while the wind carried our ships closer together. The *Pequod*, I saw when it came near enough, was old and crusty and very strange, with the ropes wrapped around pins made from whale teeth and whalebones substituting for various wooden pieces. It had a large crew.

Rachel raised her speaking tube and hollered again. "Well, hast you? I mean, hast thou? Seen the white whale."

"Of course not, silly!" Elizabeth hollered back. "We're not a whaler. And it's *your* whale! Keep looking."

"Thanks, anyway," hollered Rachel. "Hey, you should watch out."

"What for?" hollered Elizabeth.

The ships edged closer and closer, until someone with extraordinary long arms—Andre, say—could almost touch the whalebones on the other ship. The crews on both ships moved the sails around (and I ducked); soon we were sailing alongside each other.

"Listen," said Rachel—we were close enough together now

that she didn't need the trumpet—"we spoke to a ship's captain a few leagues back who told me Jonathan Rigby's looking for you. Something about you guys taking something he thinks belongs to him."

"How would he know about that?" I asked.

"Seagulls, presumably," said Rachel.

"Seagulls?" I echoed.

"Yes, he has quite a colony of them, from various literary sources," said Rachel. "His birds are surprisingly capable."

They would have to be, if they could spy on us like that.

"You know where he's at?" asked Andre. "Or which ship he's sailing?"

"Could be anywhere by now. The captain didn't say."

"Okay," said Elizabeth. "Thanks for the heads-up. Good luck finding that whale."

"A fair wind to you."

"And to you," said Elizabeth.

Our ships tacked apart, and the *Pequod* shrank quickly out of view.

"I'm not all that surprised Rigby's chasing us," said Andre.

"Yeah," said Elizabeth. "I bet that means we're on the right track."

We sailed on for a long time, following the compass through blustery weather and still, sunny seas. We saw flying fish and phosphorescence, sharks and porpoises, the occasional sail and the occasional whale—though not the great white one Rachel was looking for.

In that strange world of nonlinear time, it was hard to tell how long we had been sailing. Time didn't exactly pass, it just sort of *hovered*. I wondered if this was how the ghosts felt, suspended in time.

That made me miss Kitty. She would have enjoyed this trip when she was alive, with the swimming and sailing—although she wouldn't have wanted me to climb the rigging or swim behind the ship. I could imagine her worrying about sharks. It would have been useful to have her along as a ghost, though, to whip up the wind when it died down. She seemed very far away from me now.

When the sun or the moon came out for long enough, sometimes we would read—I'd brought along Cousin Hepzibah's copy of the unfinished novel our ancestors came from, and when I finished that, I read some Poe and Hawthorne stories I found in the cabin. Sometimes we got hungry, and one of us would cook up a meal in the galley, dried peas and salt pork and ship's biscuit. Sometimes we would pass suddenly from a patch of noon to a patch of night and take turns slinging up our hammocks in the cabin. We took turns at the tiller, too, steering the ship according to the haunted compass—all of us except Elizabeth, of course. I started to get good at sailing.

I wondered whether my parents were worrying about me. I wondered whether Kitty was worrying about me but decided not to worry about it. We weren't about to turn back, so there was nothing to do but go forward.

One morning, or at least in a point in time that felt like morning, Cole was practicing climbing up the single mast, against the orders of Andre, who considered himself the captain.

"Of course I'm the captain," Andre explained. "It's the repository's ship, and Libbet can't be captain—not with her sense of direction. Get down."

"Aye, aye, Captain," said Cole, ignoring him and climbing farther up.

"Come on, Cole. Get down from there. If you mess up the rigging, we'll be in it deep."

"You just don't like anybody to be taller than you," said Cole. He put the spyglass to his eye and shouted, "Land ho!"

"Cole, I mean it. Quit messing around," said Andre.

"No, really. Land seriously ho."

"You sure it's not just a cloud?" I asked.

"Nope, an island. Straight ahead. Right where your compass is pointing."

CHAPTER TWENTY-FOUR

Broken Isle

Glaring white beaches ringed the island, and a tuft of green trees stuck straight up in the middle like a feather headdress. A rocky scar to the east looked as though something had hacked off a huge chunk of land: an earthquake, or maybe a giant's ax. That must be what gave Broken Isle its name.

We sailed around to the northern end and dropped anchor in a sandy cove. The air here was soft and warm. We had already taken off our coats and sweaters. Now we rolled up our pants legs, hung our shoes around our necks by the laces, put on our backpacks, and splashed ashore.

"Now what?" asked Cole, wiggling his toes in the sand. "Ask the compass."

"Well, compass?" I said. "Where did Red Tom Tempest bury his treasure?" The compass swung eagerly toward the densely wooded interior. "It wants us to go up there," I said, pointing.

"Time to get our bearings," said Andre. "Find the best path up."

"Your job. I don't have any bearings," Elizabeth pointed out.

"Good one, Libbet! Just stick close."

A freshwater stream ran down to the beach from the interior of the island. We followed it upstream along a path beside it that seemed to have been made by animals. I hoped they weren't the carnivorous kind.

It was steamy in the jungle and heavy going, especially for Andre, who had to walk half bent over to keep from banging his head. Thick roots grew across the path. My backpack made my back sweaty. Whenever we tripped, we heard chuckles and hoots high above us, as if something in the trees found us funny. Monkeys? Parrots? Ghosts?

There were definitely parrots around—we often caught a red flash of wing or tail, followed by a burst of squawks and a downpour of nutshells. Phinny must have come this way a couple of centuries ago. I imagined him looking for a parrot to bring home to Windy as a pet.

Cole picked up something mango-yellow that the birds dropped. "What is this? It's kind of good."

"You're not *eating* that? Gross!" I said.

"It's perfectly safe—the birds are eating it too, and they're fine."

"That's why it's gross! Half-chewed parrot leftovers."

"Well, I'm sick of salt pork! Try some. It's good."

Elizabeth caught a piece the next time the parrots flew by. "Cole's right, it's good. Kind of like a cross between a banana and a papaya."

The forest got noisier, with a hissing, crashing sound that made it hard to understand each other's consonants. Soon we came to the source of the noise: a waterfall. Our path beside it fanned upward and faded out in what looked like a green wall.

"We supposed to go up *there*?" said Andre.

I consulted the compass. "Looks like it."

He shrugged. "Here goes, then." With his long arms and legs, he soon disappeared into the shaking green wall.

"Good thing I practiced climbing on the boat," said Cole, following him. Elizabeth started up the steep, clifflike slope after him.

I waited for her to get up a few yards, then took a deep breath and pulled myself up. Thick vines and tree roots covered the steep slope, with plenty of rocks poking out for footholds. It was like climbing on a rope net.

Halfway up, something heavy, wet, and soft hit my head. I whipped around, startled. It was just one of those yellow fruits, growing on a vine. Balancing carefully, I picked a bunch of them and dropped them down my shirt.

When I reached the top, Cole and Andre pulled me up the last few feet by the arms. "Whoa, Spooky, what happened to you? Did you swallow a snake?" said Cole, pointing to my shirt front.

I fished one of the fruits out of my shirt. "Clean and parrot-free. Want some?" I took a bite. Elizabeth was right—they were sort of like a banana and a papaya, only tarter and juicier. I found I had been thirsty. I ate two.

"Now where?" asked Andre. We were standing on a ridge, with a tall hill in front of us. With our backs to the hill we could see the ocean far below us through the trees.

I consulted my compass. It bobbed around in a slow circle,

the tip pointing downward. "Hm," I said. "I think we're here. Did anyone remember to bring shovels?"

Andre had three folding shovels in his backpack. It was hard work digging in the humid heat, but it went fast with the four of us—or maybe it just felt as though time wasn't passing because the sun wasn't moving. We took turns digging; the one without the shovel sat on the edge of the ledge, scanning the horizon through the trees for sails.

I was standing up to my chin in the hole, heaving dirt over my head and thinking about what a workout my triceps were getting, when Andre hit something hard. "Here!" he shouted.

Elizabeth, who'd been taking her turn as lookout, rushed over. "Wait!" she shouted.

"What?" asked Andre.

"Are we sure it's safe? Pirate treasure can be haunted. Sometimes they bury a prisoner alive, to guard it. Or they lay a curse. Like in that Stowe story, 'Captain Kidd's Money,' where the devil drags the gold down to Hell, and they barely escape getting dragged down with it."

"Isn't it a little late to worry about that?" I asked.

Cole looked stubborn. "I don't know about you, but I'm not quitting now. We've come too far. I'm going to risk it."

"Me too." I bit the earth with my shovel blade. Soon we'd cleared the top of an ironbound chest. "Look, no demons," I said.

"So far," said Elizabeth.

We scrabbled away at the hole until we'd cleared the whole chest.

"Is this what you saw the ghost holding?" asked Cole.

"Not sure. This might be bigger. The one I saw was all glowy and transparent, so it's hard to compare," I said. "How are we going to get it out?"

"I brought rope," said Andre.

It took us a great deal of coordinated levering with fallen branches, cascading dirt, banged elbows, and rope burns before we managed to haul the chest out of the hole.

"Come on! Let's open it!" said Cole.

"I expect it's locked," said Elizabeth.

It was. Seven times. There were built-in locks on three sides and hasps with heavy iron padlocks, one on each short side and two on the front.

"Well, Andre? Did you bring an ax, too?" asked Cole.

"No. And if we break it open, how are we going to get the gold down to the ship?"

"How are we going to get the *chest* down to the ship?" I said. "That thing's heavy!"

"Yeah—but that's a good thing," said Andre. "Heavy means lots of gold."

"I'm not so sure," said Elizabeth, pushing a muddy lock of hair out of her eyes with an even muddier hand. "Shouldn't that much gold be even heavier?"

"Maybe it's not coins. Maybe it's pearls and rubies and diamonds," said Cole.

I went over to the stream to rinse my hands and face. There was a clear view over the waterfall, all the way down to the beach. "Whatever's in it, we need to get it to the ship fast," I said. "It looks like that Rigby guy found us."

• • •

People assume it's easier to go downhill than uphill, but that's not always true. Not when you're carrying a pirate's chest made of oak and iron and covered in slippery mud. Especially not when the chest is so heavy that it takes at least two people to carry it, and the slope is so steep that you need all your hands and feet free to hang onto roots and branches. And extra-especially not when you're racing against time to get back to your ship before a rival finds you with the loot.

We reached the beach with no broken bones and only one turned ankle (Cole's). But we were too late. A big, black ship was hovering just beyond the cove, and a boat was rowing toward us.

"Uh-oh, Libbet! Is that what I think?" said Andre.

"Large hermaphrodite brig. Dutch build. Black paint. Tawdry gilt figurehead. Yes, I'm afraid so," said Elizabeth. "Hurry up! We need to get under way right now or we'll never outrun them." She and Andre began dragging the chest as fast as they could down the beach. I pushed from behind.

"You're afraid it's *what*?" asked Cole, limping beside us.

"The Dutch trader from *The Narrative of Arthur Gordon Pym*," panted Elizabeth. "The same Poe novel as our ship. It's a version of the *Flying Dutchman*, from the legends."

"What legends?" I asked.

"Lots of legends," said Andre.

"The *Flying Dutchman* is a legendary ghost ship sailed by corpses," Elizabeth explained. "It can never land, so it just sails around forever. It shows up all over the place in literature. The Dublin Repository in Ireland has the version from the Thomas

Moore poem, and the Alba Repository in Scotland has the one from the Sir Walter Scott poem—it's from a footnote to 'Rokeby.' It's one of my favorite examples of footnote objects. Another one is—"

"Less talking, Libbet. More pulling," urged Andre.

I redoubled my efforts too. My heels dug deep into the sand as I pushed. "Well, so what's the problem?" I panted. "If they can't land, they can't hurt us."

"They can stop us from leaving, though. We're outmanned," said Elizabeth. "They have a vast crew. And they're all dead, so they can't be killed. And we can't outsail a hermaphrodite brig."

"What's a hermaphrodite brig?"

"It means they're using two kinds of rigging. It makes the ship incredibly fast and maneuverable."

The dead *Dutchman* did have a very complicated system of sails: some square, some triangular, with two masts. The sails themselves, though, didn't look so hot. They were tattered and threadbare, with the sun glaring through holes. And the breeze from the sea carried a stench of rot so bad it belonged in the Lovecraft Corpus.

Cole made a face. "What's that smell?"

"The crew. Did I mention they're dead?"

We reached the low-tide mark and were just dragging the chest into the water when the rowboat from the hermaphrodite brig drew near the beach.

There was something very strange about the dead sailors. Stranger than just being dead, I mean. Five or six big seagulls were sitting on each corpse. At first I thought they were eating the bodies—disgusting as it sounds, seagulls will eat rotting garbage, so why not dead sailors? But then I saw they were actually pulling on the corpses' muscles, moving them like life-sized marionettes. The birds were using the corpses to do the rowing.

A familiar figure hopped out of the rowboat, timing his leap against the waves and holding his smoking pipe over his head to keep it dry. The smell of the smoke mixed horribly with the stench of the rotting sailors at the oars. He frowned at the spray that had splashed his butter-colored linen jacket and matching Bermuda shorts, then shifted his frown to us. "I'll take that, if you please," he said, and pointed to the chest.

It was Feathertop.

"Why should we give it to you?" said Cole.

"Because it belongs to my employer. You found it on his island. Without permission, I might add."

"It does not," said Cole. "Our great-great-great-great-granduncle buried it here. Our great-great-great-great-aunt sent us to get it. It belongs to us."

"The laws governing supernatural salvage are very clear," said Feathertop. "They favor my employer. His island, his chest."

"Not as clear as all that," said Elizabeth. "Sukie and Cole have at least as good a case. Their ghosts, their prophesy, their plunder."

"Well, perhaps. But there are only four of you." He waved his hand at the teeming, reeking ship.

Elizabeth said, "We could just stay here until you leave. Your sailors can't come ashore."

"You could, true. But I expect you'll get tired of parrot fruit sooner or later. And after a year or two, the children will probably begin to miss their parents. If you're so keen on keeping our property, we might strike a bargain. You have several items we would be happy to consider taking in exchange."

Andre called to the rowboat, "Yo, Rigby! You down with these gangster tactics?"

A salt-and-pepper head poked out from behind the corpses: the suave man from the flea market. "Feathertop is doing a fine job representing my interests," he called back. "He offered you a trade. Why not take it?"

"We would happily accept the Yellow Sign, for example," said Feathertop.

"I don't have the Yellow Sign anymore," I said. "And I wouldn't give it to you if I did."

"Well, your Hawthorne broom, then. That would be a fantastic bargain for *you*—the chest is sure to be worth much more."

"I'm not trading away my heirlooms. Anyway, I didn't bring the broom."

"Stop! Look!" yelled Cole, pointing. "They got our ship!"

It was true. While we were arguing with Feathertop, a boatload of corpses had landed on the *Ariel* and were busily hoisting the sails.

"I'm sure you would hate to be stranded here," said Feathertop. He stepped closer to me. "I can smell haunted objects on you. What have you got? I'll just take a look, shall I?" I drew back, but he stepped even closer and stuck his hand in my pocket.

I screamed and hit him. Cole and Andre ran at him. Feathertop took a deep drag on his pipe and blew the smoke straight in Andre's face, then stuck out his foot daintily in front of Cole. Both guys fell sprawling in the sand, Cole clutching his injured ankle and Andre choking for breath.

"Cole! Andre!" I screamed.

Feathertop took another deep drag on his pipe and reached for the cord around my neck, the one my sister's whistle hung from. I twisted away to avoid the noisome blast of smoke, but before I could stop him, he had yanked the whistle free.

"Well, what have we here?" he said. "This summons a spirit, doesn't it? I could use a spirit servant."

"Give me that! That's mine! You can't have it!" I sounded like a four-year-old. I wished I *was* a four-year-old. Nothing like this would have happened when I was four and my sister was around to protect me. I wished I hadn't told her to leave me alone.

"Jonathan! I can't believe you're doing this!" Elizabeth yelled. She was fishing desperately in her bag for something.

Rigby had jumped into the water—it came up to his chest—and was half swimming, half wading toward us. "All's fair in collecting," he said. "Anyway, *you're* the ones who are trying to steal from *me*."

I grappled with Feathertop, trying to get the whistle back.

Then several things happened fast. Feathertop got the whistle to his lips and blew. A stream of evil, shrieking smoke wailed through the whistle. The sound was louder and deadlier and more horrifying than anything I'd ever heard. In one of those abrupt, disorienting time shifts, the sun blinked out of the sky. And through the smoky, crepuscular gloaming, a phantom came streaming. My sister.

Never before had I seen her so vast and furious. She was unimaginably vivid—and everyone could see her! She might have been any dead horror screaming for vengeance.

"Get the box!" Feathertop commanded her.

Kitty made it clear that he couldn't command her, and the only thing she would be *getting* was Feathertop.

The two of them drew back, then rushed at each other.

I wouldn't have thought anything could hurt a ghost, but apparently something in Feathertop's pipe smoke gave him powers that reached even beyond the grave. But my sister had been summoned by a blast of the same infernal smoke that filled his lungs. They were well matched.

At dusk, a ghost bleeds black. A fiend bleeds glowing ichor. And the agonized cries of each can shatter wood. Branches fell all about us, splintering as they hit the sand.

The worst thing about their fight was how familiar it seemed. I'd watched Kitty fight like that on playgrounds all through my childhood, defending me from bullies, real and imagined. This was a horrible, unstoppable parody of something I'd loved and relied on.

"Jonathan! Curb your creature!" Elizabeth screamed, still fishing in her bag.

"Curb yours!" screamed Rigby.

"She's not my creature!" Elizabeth answered.

"She's not a *creature*! She's my *sister*!" I screamed.

"Both of you, stop!" Rigby yelled, grabbing at Kitty. His hands went through her, but when she cuffed him away, he went flying across the beach. He crashed into a pile of seaweed and lay dazed.

Elizabeth found what she was looking for in her purse and held it out. "Feathertop! Here!" she screamed.

Feathertop turned his head toward her. She was holding up a mirror.

His eyes went wide. Then he changed. In the dim light I watched his cheeks harden into ridges, his snappy suit fall into rags. The pipe faded and went out, then tumbled to the sand. Suddenly nothing was left of Feathertop but a heap of lifeless objects: a pumpkin-headed scarecrow, a broomstick, and an old clay pipe.

I stared. What had happened to him?

Kitty wailed in wordless exaltation. With a high-pitched shriek like a fighter plane, she flew over Rigby's rowboat. As she passed, the corpses tumbled into the bottom of the boat beneath her, and a cloud of birds flew upward, radiantly white in the gloom. The corpses on the *Ariel* all scrambled into their boat and started pulling on their oars, but before they could reach the Dutch trader, Kitty flew over them shrieking, and the same thing happened: Corpses collapsed; birds flew away.

We all stared, dazed. Rigby sat up, rubbing his head.

"What happened to the corpses?" said Cole.

"Can't you stop her? She's scaring off my gulls!" yelled Rigby.

"Not our problem," said Andre. "You're the one who summoned her. Your creature did, anyway."

"But I'm going to be stranded here!"

"Oh, the irony," said Elizabeth.

The moon rose, blazing quickly up the sky, and the corpses on the mother ship leapt into action. Elizabeth was right about the ship's speed. It could outpace a ghost, apparently. Soon the ship had slipped beneath the horizon, my sister streaming after it. Her howls echoed back to us for a long time after they'd both vanished.

CHAPTER TWENTY-FIVE

A Dead Man's Chest

Cole breathed. "What just happened?"

Kitty's blue whistle glinted in the moonlight next to Feathertop's remains. I picked it up. "When Feathertop blew my whistle, he summoned my sister. After that, I have no idea."

"What is all this trash?" Cole nudged the pumpkin with the toe of his shoe. It made a disgusting squelching noise.

"Careful with that!" said Rigby. He bent over the pile of stuff and rummaged through it with gingerly distaste, picking out an old clay pipe and a broom that looked a lot like mine.

"What happened to Feathertop?" said Cole. "How could a person turn into all *this*?"

"Feathertop wasn't a person, exactly," said Elizabeth. "He was a satiric literary construction, a sort of Pygmalion variant."

"A what?"

"It's a Greek myth about a sculptor who brings his statue to life. This is one of Hawthorne's versions. He was kind of obsessed with the myth. Did you ever read his story 'Feathertop'?"

We shook our heads.

"It's like a snarky twist on Pygmalion. A witch builds a scarecrow out of a pumpkin, some old clothes, and her broom. She likes him so much she decides to bring him to life, so she gives him her pipe to smoke."

"*That* pipe?" I asked, pointing to Rigby's hand.

"Yes. It's the jewel of my collection," said Rigby.

"The pipe has demonic powers," said Elizabeth. "Whoever controls it can summon a fiend to light it with an infernal ember and keep it filled with diabolical tobacco."

We all looked at Rigby. "You smoke diabolical tobacco lit by hellfire? I guess that explains your challenged ethics," I said.

It was hard to tell in the moonlight, but I thought Rigby looked offended. "Oh, like *you* don't fly around on diabolical broomsticks? Anyway, I don't smoke it *myself*," he said. "I made my scarecrow smoke it. And there's nothing wrong with *my* ethics. *You're* the one who's stealing from *me*."

"Whatever," said Cole. "How does the pipe turn a scarecrow into a creep?"

Elizabeth said, "In the Hawthorne story, the smoke turns the scarecrow into a dandy—the kind of guy who wears expensive clothes and tries to worm his way into high society. He gets his name from the feather in his hat. But whenever the tobacco runs out, Feathertop has to summon the demon to refill it and light it, and if the demon's not quick enough, he starts to change back into a scarecrow."

I had seen Feathertop start to change, I realized, that time his pipe went out at the flea market. "So what happened here? Did the pipe somehow go out?" I asked.

"No. I showed him my mirror. It reflected his true self. He's so vain, whenever he sees his true form, he throws down the pipe in despair and turns back into a scarecrow."

"Which is a total pain, thank you very much," said Rigby. "Where am I going to get another pumpkin on this forsaken island?"

"Seriously, Jonathan? You threaten to strand us on a desert island, you sic your creature on us, and then you complain when I disable him?" Elizabeth rolled her eyes.

"Hey, *your* creature attacked first."

I said, "I keep telling you, that's my *sister*! She's *nobody's* creature!" I wondered where Kitty had gone and when I would see her again. I was way too freaked out by her new, fierce vividness to summon her now, though.

"Well, she drove off my seagulls, and it's going to take forever to find them, and who knows where my ship is by now," said Rigby. "Can you give me a lift back? Just drop me at any annex port along the railroad line."

"You're kidding! Why shouldn't we leave you here, like you were going to do to us?" asked Andre.

"You won't do that. I know you and Elizabeth," said Rigby. "You're far too nice."

I said, "Even if we take you back, we're keeping the treasure."

"No, you're not. The treasure's mine," said Rigby.

"Bye, then," I said, grabbing a corner of the chest. "Come on, Cole, help me get this thing onto the *Ariel*."

"Okay, okay, we'll split the treasure," said Rigby. "Half for me, half for you two. You know it's my island!"

Cole and I looked at each other. After all, Rigby had a point. "A third for each of us," I said.

"Done," said Rigby. "That looks heavy. Let me give you a hand."

Back on the *Ariel*, Cole and I wanted to dump the corpses overboard, but Rigby argued that they were a valuable part of his collection and would be perfectly usable once he'd reassembled his seagulls. We agreed to let him pile the corpses in the Dutch trader's rowboat and tow it behind us.

I regretted the decision as soon as we started sailing. In a sailboat, the wind generally comes more or less from behind. We spent the whole trip holding our noses.

To my surprise, Jonathan Rigby turned out to be a great sailing companion. He taught Cole and me how to tie seventeen different kinds of knots, kept us entertained with sea shanties, and knew the names of all the different kinds of seaweed.

"You're kind of fun for a monster," I said when he showed me how to attract flying fish by threading little bits of parrot fruit on a string—and how to drop them gently back in the water before they suffocated.

"I'm not a monster myself. I just collect them," he told me.

The trip home seemed to take far less time than the trip out. Maybe it was the prevailing winds or the ocean currents, maybe just the pattern of daytime and nighttime. Or maybe there was some kink in the geography, and the way back actually *was* shorter than the way out. Whatever the reason, the Flint compass brought us back to our port of origin in what felt like no time at all.

• • •

Even after we landed, the reek of the corpses clung to our clothes and hair. "No offense, Spooky, but you stink," said Cole. "Stinky Spooky."

I made a face at him. "Very mature. You're not exactly a bouquet of roses yourself, you know."

Back onshore, Jonathan's acquisitive, competitive streak came roaring back. He wanted to buy my whistle, my Hawthorne broom, my compass. To his credit, though, he didn't threaten to drown me or strand me when I said no. He just argued. "What do you need the compass for? You already found the treasure."

We'd borrowed a wheelbarrow from one of the warehouses down by the docks and were taking turns pushing it up the brick streets. It rattled so hard I kept biting my tongue.

"That's assuming this *is* the treasure. We don't actually know what's in this chest. How are we going to get it open?" I said.

"You mean you don't have the key?" Jonathan sounded pleased.

"I don't know if there even is one. It's not mentioned in the book, and the ghosts didn't say anything about it, either."

"I bet Doc can help," said Andre. "We've got all kinds of keys in our collection."

We reached the station just as our train was pulling in. "Quick! It's bad luck to miss a spectral train," said Elizabeth, starting to run.

I pushed the wheelbarrow after them as hard as I could. "How did the train know we were coming?" I panted.

"Spectral trains are like that," said Andre, scrambling aboard.

We barely had time to pull the doors shut behind us before the train belched smoke and clattered into motion.

Jonathan Rigby spent the whole ride staring out the window looking green.

"You okay?" Andre asked. "You think you're going to throw up? The washroom's that way."

"How come you collect ships if you get motion sickness?" Cole asked.

Jonathan sniffed at them. "The problem's not my stomach, thanks for your kind concern. It's your collection." He waved his hand at the window. "I can't believe you snagged the House of Usher. That should be mine!" He whipped his head around to watch the castle disappear behind a hill. I thought he looked less about to throw up than about to breathe fire. But when he turned around again, the scene up ahead didn't seem to make him feel any better. "Oh! Is that Bly? How on *earth* did you get your claws on *Bly*?" He actually gnashed his teeth.

It was a relief when we pulled into Lost Penn Station, where Dr. Rust was waiting for us with Griffin. Andre tilted the chest down the train steps.

"Oh, good—you found it!" said the librarian.

"Ruff," agreed the dog.

"Doc, do you know if we have the key to this chest?" asked Elizabeth.

"I'm pretty sure we don't."

"Can you think of anything else we could use to open it, then?"

"Hm . . . let me think. The Golden Key won't work—it's in the wrong genre. . . . The Key to All Mythologies is just a big, useless joke. . . . We have tons of skeleton keys, but they always lead to such bad puns. . . . Oh! I know. What about Leo's multifunctional tool?"

"Great idea," said Andre. "He upstairs?"

"No, down here, testing some ectoplasmic trackers he's been working on. I passed him a little while ago on Eldritch Street, on the Lowest East Side. He's probably still there."

"Is it far?" I asked. My arms were aching from pushing that chest around.

"Yes and no. It depends how you go. You could take the haunted hansom from 'Consequences'—that might be easier. You and Cole, take the chest with you. The rest of us can meet you on Eldritch Street."

"What's 'Consequences'?"

"A Willa Cather story. It's one of those ones where the ghost is really the—"

"Doc! Spoiler alert!" interrupted Andre.

"Right. Sorry. Anyway, the hansom should be able to take you to the Lowest East Side."

Andre helped us lug the chest to a row of weird-looking vehicles waiting outside the station. The haunted hansom was a small horse carriage drawn by a bony gray horse. The driver wore a red flannel scarf and a broken hat, which he tipped to Elizabeth with the handle of his switch. "Eldritch Street, right away!" he said, and we rattled off through a strangely swirling streetscape.

"This is kind of creepy," whispered Cole.

"Creepier than everything else?"

"No, but still."

I secretly agreed and was fighting the impulse to reach out for Cole's hand when we clattered into a broad street crowded with ghostly pushcarts. Blurred phantoms leaned out of upper windows of tenements howling, "Moiiiiishe! Miiiiiickeeeeeey!! Saaaaaaalvatoooooore!!! HOWWWWWWIEEEEEE!!! Ya forgot yer MITTTTTTTENNNNS!!"

Our cabbie pulled on the reins, the bony horse shuddered to a stop, and we stepped out, lugging the chest after us. Apparently either Elizabeth had already paid him or haunted cabbies don't expect tips, because before we could get our bearings, he had clicked his tongue at the old gray horse and vanished into the swirl.

A guy had been bending over one of the ghostly pushcarts, waving an instrument through it. The instrument consisted of a wand attached by a red cord to a metal box covered with dials and buttons and switches; as it passed through the pushcart, it let out a burst of beeps.

He straightened up at the sound of our carriage and looked at us. He had a long face, with a curl of dark brown hair falling into his warm brown eyes. He seemed around college age, medium height and neatly built, as if an engineer had taken some trouble to get him right.

"Hello! You look real," he said, pushing the curl out of his eyes.

"Thanks. You do too," I said.

"Hang on, let me just check." He adjusted some knobs on his machine, then waved the wand over my head. It beeped again. I jumped back.

He waved it in Cole's face. It beeped again. "Hey!" objected Cole.

"Schist, that's strange!" said the guy. "You're both definitely real, but I'm getting a positive reading for ectoplasm. You're not partially disembodied, are you?" He poked Cole in the chest with the wand.

"Seriously, quit it!" said Cole.

"No disembodiment, your chest seems solid," said the guy. "You're not off lying in a coma somewhere, are you? Or fractionally dead?"

"Of course not! But *you* will be, if you don't quit poking me with that thing."

"I'm sorry. You're right, that was rude of me. It's just such an anomalous reading—I can't understand it."

"Our ancestors are fictional," I said. "Some of them, anyway. Could that explain it?"

"Fascinating. Yes, maybe. Do you have a few minutes? I would love to get you into the lab and run some tests."

Suddenly the sky went dark. The air swirled with bats, their high-pitched, skittery pips and clicks weaving confusingly among the howls of the phantom tenement tenants. I ducked instinctively and put my arms over my head.

When I straightened up, the bats were gone, but Dr. Rust, Elizabeth, Andre, and Griffin were standing on the sidewalk.

Cousin Hepzibah was there too, sitting very upright in an antique wheelchair, the kind made of oak with a caned back and seat and big wooden wheels. Andre was pushing it. Jonathan Rigby arrived seconds later, riding his Hawthorne broom.

"Oh, good. You've met already," said Dr. Rust.

"We haven't, actually," said the young man. "Friends of yours, Doc?"

"Sukie O'Dare and Cole Farley," said Dr. Rust. "Friends of the repository. They have a favor to ask you. Sukie and Cole, this is Leo Novikov. Leo's doing great things in literary-material mechanics."

"Oh, I just like to mess around with spare parts," said the young man modestly. "What's the favor?"

Andre pointed to our treasure chest. "You think you can get that open?"

"I don't see why not. It isn't cursed, is it?"

"Not that we know of."

Leo nodded, frowning. He walked around the chest, leaning over to inspect the locks, then adjusted some dials on the machine and waved the wand in a complicated pattern. Nothing beeped. "Yeah, okay. I'll see what I can do."

He pulled what looked like a Swiss Army knife out of his pocket and opened one of the tools. It looked like a teeny, tiny hand. He inserted it into the first lock, frowning with concentration. After a few seconds, the lock popped open. "It seems pretty straightforward, just a little phantasmic resistance. And some rust," he said, moving on to the next lock.

When the locks were all open, he stood back. We all looked

at each other, holding our breath. I wished I could summon Windy and Phinny. I was sure they would want to see this.

After a minute, Jonathan Rigby cleared his throat and offered, "Sukie, Cole—will you do the honors?"

Cole and I stepped forward and each grabbed an end of the lid.

"Here goes nothing," said Cole. "One, two, three!"

Together, hearts pounding, we lifted the lid.

The chest was empty.

CHAPTER TWENTY-SIX

The Sullivan Looking Glass

"How can it be empty?" I raged. "The compass is supposed to find the treasure! What's *wrong* with it? Is it broken? Is it lying?"

"It might not be the compass's fault," said Dr. Rust gently. "What did you ask it? The exact words."

I tried to remember. "'Find Broken Isle,' I think."

"Well, it did that," said Andre.

"I'm sorry, Sukie," said Elizabeth. "It's my fault—I should have warned you. Magic objects can be perversely literal-minded. You have to pick your words really, really carefully."

"What about *on* the island?" said Cole. "It took us straight to the chest."

"Sukie probably told it to find where they buried the treasure or something like that, not to find the treasure itself," said Andre. "Right, Sukie?"

I nodded. "Yeah, something like that."

"I'm sorry—I should have paid more attention," said Andre.

"Ask it again," said Jonathan. "Ask it to find Red Tom's treasure this time."

"You know none of the treasure's yours, Jonathan, right? Since it's not on your island," said Cole.

Jonathan waved his hand in what might have been agreement—or not. "Let's just find it. Ask the compass, Sukie."

I shut my eyes. I felt so tired and disappointed and defeated. And mad. All that work and hope, and no treasure! I couldn't bear the thought of Windy's disappointment. She'd been waiting so long.

Pulling myself together, I opened my eyes and said, "Compass, find Red Tom's treasure."

But the compass just turned indecisively, wobbling here and there.

"The treasure must be dispersed. It's not one, single treasure anymore," said Dr. Rust. "Phineas probably spent it."

"I think that's right," said Elizabeth. "Flint talks about the *Pretty Polly* capturing slave ships and setting the captives free. I wouldn't be surprised if Phineas gave them gold from Red Tom's treasure to start their new lives with. Or to pay for passage home to Africa, maybe. None of that's in the unfinished manuscript, but maybe it was in her notes or her outline."

"Then why did Windy's ghost tell Sukie to find Phinny's treasure?" asked Cole.

It struck me like a blow to the stomach. "She didn't. She told me to find *her* treasure."

"Ask the compass *that*, then," said Jonathan. "Go on!"

"I don't think it's going to work," said Elizabeth. "It's Red Tom's compass. I doubt it knows about Windy's treasure. Whatever that turns out to be."

She was right. "Find Windy Toogood's treasure," I told it. "Hepzibah Thorne Toogood's treasure."

I even added, "Please." But the compass didn't respond.

It was all too much. My dead sister, my lost house, my cursed family. Then the new chapter beginning: the broom, the compass, the ship, the trip, the climb, the corpses, the seagulls, my furious sister—I could still feel her rage zinging at the edges of my attention. All that vast bustle seemed to be pointing to some glorious, shining climax. And then this.

This empty box.

I sat down on the curb, ignoring the ghostly filth—phantom corn husks and newspaper scraps and worse things—and put my head in my hands, trying not to cry.

Someone sat down next to me and put an arm around me. "Cheer up, Sukie. It's not over yet." It was Andre.

"It *is*. The compass doesn't work. We'll never find the treasure," I muttered to my shoes.

"Nonsense," said another voice—Dr. Rust. "We're librarians. When we don't find what we're looking for in the first place we look, we don't give up. We keep looking."

Andre was poking something at me under my bent shoulders. I took it: a tissue, crumpled but clean. I blew my nose and leaned against him. "Okay," I said. "Where? Where do we keep looking?"

"Jonathan, you got any useful treasure maps?" asked Andre.

Jonathan Rigby laughed. "If I did, don't you think I would have found the treasure already?"

"Fair point."

"What about the Sullivan looking glass?" suggested Dr. Rust.

"Oh, now *that's* a thought!" said Elizabeth.

"What's the Sullivan looking glass?"

"From a Harriet Beecher Stowe story," said Dr. Rust. "It's a prognosticator. The heroine uses it to find a missing will. She looks in the mirror and sees herself in a strange room opening a drawer in a cabinet and taking out some papers, and she knows that one of the papers is the missing will. Maybe if you look in the mirror, you'll see yourself finding the missing treasure."

"There's a problem, though," said Elizabeth. "The girl in the story has the gift of seeing. She was born with a veil over her face—a caul. You weren't born with a caul, were you, Sukie?"

"I was very premature," I said. "I don't know about a caul."

Cousin Hepzibah said, "Yes, you were a caul birth. So was I. It's common in our family."

"Awesome!" said Andre, hopping up and pulling me with him. "Let's go check out the Sullivan mirror."

Jonathan straddled his broom. "Which way?"

"The Lovecraft Corpus. And you're not coming. I wouldn't trust you in there as far as Ms. Thorne could throw you," said Andre.

"You can't mean that! I agreed to hand over two-thirds of my treasure, out of the goodness of my heart!"

"Oh, let him come. He'll be okay—with Griffin keeping an eye on him," said Elizabeth.

"Arp," said Griffin, leaping to Jonathan's side. Nobody in their right mind would try anything with those gigantic teeth in biting distance.

I didn't like the Lovecraft Corpus any better on the third visit. The stink was even worse than Jonathan's corpses, and I had a horrible feeling that something was following me—something vast, fierce, and vengeful. The underfoot squishing didn't help.

"How I adore this place," said Jonathan. "I could stay here forever."

"One false step, and you might," said Andre.

"You repositorians. Such a sense of humor," said Jonathan.

Soon we came to a patch of gloom where shiny objects glinted around us—mirrors.

I peeked into one and screamed. A malicious face was staring back at me: an old lady, cruel and covetous, scowling with hatred and misery. "Who is *that*?" I choked. "That's not *me*, is it?"

Everybody stopped. Elizabeth peeked into the mirror. "Oh, that's just Aunt Harriet, from 'The Southwest Chamber,'" she said. "By Mary Wilkins Freeman. Aunt Harriet won't hurt you. She doesn't like people messing with her stuff, that's all. Even after she's dead."

I tore my eyes away from the scowling lady. "What a lot of mirrors," I said.

"Yes, they're very popular in supernatural fiction," said Dr. Rust.

Griffin gave a low growl.

"Try not to look into them," said Andre. "Some of them

are portals to different dimensions. Or they can transform the viewer. You don't want to get turned evil, or haunted."

"I'm already haunted," I pointed out. Again, I wondered where Kitty was. Still chasing those evil seagulls? The longer I didn't see her, the more I worried. For years I had felt her presence hovering nearby, even when she didn't manifest. Now, though . . . now I felt *something*, that was for sure. Something scary. But it didn't feel like Kitty.

"Are all the mirrors dangerous?" asked Cole.

"This one's okay—it just shows invisible spirits," said Andre, pointing to a large mirror in a mahogany frame.

I edged around to peek in.

I was right. Something *was* following me—something both as familiar as my own hand and completely unknown. A vast, fiery shape stood behind me, hair and eyes blazing red. It looked as if some evil genius had sculpted Kitty out of smoke and flame.

"Kitty?" I cried, whipping around, but all I saw behind me was the sinister gloom of the Lovecraft Corpus.

"You okay?" asked Andre.

"Yeah, fine." It was just the lighting, I told myself. Anything would look scary here, especially a ghost. Kitty was my sister. She was nothing to be afraid of.

I didn't look in that mirror again, though.

"Where's the Sullivan looking glass?" asked Cole.

"Here," said Dr. Rust. "Sukie?"

I pulled myself together and turned. I saw a tall mirror, the kind the people at the flea market call Venetian, with a frame made out of pieces of mirror cut into fancy shapes and engraved with scrolled patterns. We could have gotten a lot of money for it, if we'd had it in our flea market booth. And if it hadn't been haunted.

I stepped closer, peering into it in the dim light. I felt lightheaded, and everything went dim and swimmy.

Then my vision cleared, and I saw myself in the mirror. My back, though, not my face, and I wasn't in the creepy Corpus. I was in my cousin's parlor, groping at the walls next to the fireplace, pressing and tapping at the panels.

The me in the mirror must have hit a spring, because suddenly one of the panels sprang away. I saw myself reach into a dark, cavernous opening and pull something out.

"Come on, Sukie! Come on, turn around!" I urged the girl in the mirror.

As if she'd heard me, she swiveled toward me. In her arms she was holding a chest—the same one Windy's ghost had showed me. How could I have confused it with Red Tom's empty chest? This one was much smaller, with more iron bands and no locks.

"It worked! We've got to go home!" I cried. "The treasure's there! It's been there all along!"

CHAPTER TWENTY-SEVEN

Hepzibah Toogood's Treasure

When we got back to the old Thorne Mansion, my parents' truck was still gone. Judging by the sun, it was around noon. Andre glanced at the newspaper lying on our porch. "It's still Sunday. Good, we got you back early." he said.

"Sunday, as in the day after we left? But it felt like we were gone for days!" I said.

"Time's funny in the annex," said Andre. "Usually a lot longer than out here. Sometimes we even come back before we left, which can be a little inconvenient." He ducked his head under the threshold, and we all trooped down the hallway to the parlor.

I felt the panels beside the fireplace, pressing and tapping. "I think it was on this side."

"That sounded hollow," said Cole. "Right there."

I pushed on the panel. Nothing. I tapped again, pressing each corner separately. Then I tried with both hands, pushing up. I must have hit a spring, because the panel sprang away with a burst of dust.

Behind it was a dark opening.

I reached in and felt something hard and rectangular, soft with dust, and very, very cold. Carefully I pulled it out and turned to show my friends and my cousin.

For a moment, nobody could move.

"Put it down," said Andre. "That thing's got to be heavy if it's gold."

"It's not. Not that heavy," I said with a sinking feeling. I carried it over to the table and set it down gently.

We all looked at it. I think everyone else was thinking what I was thinking: another empty box.

"There's no lock," said Elizabeth.

A dank smell came from the dark hole beside the fireplace. Motes of dust rioted in a slanting sunbeam. I felt a strong presence all around me, something ghostly and concentrated. I recognized the fiery fury that I'd seen in my sister, but at a distance now. Nearer, much nearer and more urgent, something colder and older blasted out a longing so intense I thought my senses might break. Windy and Phinny.

But that wasn't all. I also felt that hard, dark, ominous presence, the one that had haunted my dreams. It felt harder than my sister at her angriest. Colder, stronger. It felt as evil as the Yellow Sign. It made me want to jam the chest back in the wall and run.

Instead, I took a deep breath and lifted the lid.

It resisted for a few long moments, then opened with a creak. The chest was not empty. Not empty at all.

Inside lay curled a tiny skeleton.

• • •

Windy and Phinny let out an exhalation of sorrow and relief so intense that everyone in the room felt it. Cole and Elizabeth gasped.

I stepped back from the coffin as Windy and Phinny converged around it, glowing gold and white, blazing with love. Phineas looked so beautiful and strong, I felt a wave of longing. He and Windy leaned over the chest together and then seemed to sink into it, their glow dimming as an eclipse dims the moon.

The hard presence let out a blast of rage and frustration that felt as if it might tear my bones apart. I sank to my knees, covering my face, but I could see the ghost through my hands: A thin man, tall, colorless, with the features of my family, emitting so much fury I thought the house must collapse.

"No, Japhet!" someone cried—Cousin Hepzibah, her voice high and strong. "You don't want to destroy your own home!"

The whole building shook. The plaster in the ceiling cracked. Bits of stone and mortar rained down in the hearth. And then the ghost was gone.

After a minute, Cole said, "So is the gold somewhere else? Do we have to start the search all over again now?"

"No, child," said Cousin Hepzibah. "Don't you see? This *is* Windy's treasure. It's Jack Toogood. Her son."

"If that's really the treasure," said Jonathan Rigby, "I relinquish my claim to a third of it."

I closed the coffin.

"I don't get it," said Cole. "Why's the baby in a box? What's the box doing in the wall? Wasn't he supposed to have drowned and been swept out to sea?"

"We'll probably never know for sure," said Elizabeth, "since Laetitia Flint never finished writing the novel. But I bet she meant to end the story something like this: When Japhet Thorne killed little Jack, he stabbed him or slit his throat, or something like that—something that left a mark on the body. He was afraid if anyone saw it, they would know what he'd done. So he hid Jack's body and said it was swept away to sea."

"That does sound like something Laetitia Flint would write," I said. "She loved blood and melodrama."

And I hated her for it. Instead of riches to rescue my parents from their problems, all we had was a bitter resolution to a sad, sad tale. If you thought about it, this whole miserable story was responsible for the Thorne family curse that killed my sister.

"What do we do with baby Jack now?" I asked. "We can't just stick him back in the wall."

"We'll bury him with his parents," said Cousin Hepzibah. "Best to do it before your parents get home. I'd rather not remind them of dead children."

For the second time that weekend, I found myself at the bottom of a pit at the top of a hill, throwing my weight behind a shovel. The ground was cold, wet, and heavy, but not frozen. My arms ached. So did the back of my throat, with tears hammering to get out. Crows watched us from a nearby weeping willow.

Griffin scrabbled in the grave, spraying dirt around. "Thanks, boy, but you're not really helping," said Andre.

"Here," said Cole. "I hit something. I think it's a coffin."

With a loud caw, a crow flew down for a closer look. Griffin growled, and it flapped a wing at him disdainfully.

Elizabeth brushed dirt away from a plaque on the long box. "Yes, it's Windy's. Let's put Jack over here, next to her."

We widened the space beside Windy's coffin, climbed out, and lowered the box into it.

"Should we say a prayer or something?" asked Cole.

We all said the Lord's Prayer, and Cousin Hepzibah recited a psalm, the one about green pastures and still waters. Then we shoveled the dirt back in the grave. Jonathan brushed it smooth with his Hawthorne broom, and we covered it with leaves.

"Look!" said Cole.

Despite the winter cold, the rosebush next to Windy's gravestone was sprouting a bud. It swelled as we watched, growing fuller and fatter until it burst into flower, red as blood, white as death. It smelled just like the Flint rose in the Poe Annex.

Then I saw Windy and Phineas standing beside the rosebush. Sunlight streamed through her, shadow through him; in her arms she held a little boy who glowed like dawn. She turned to me with what looked like my own eyes. "Thank you, Susannah," she said.

Phineas bent down and kissed me. His kiss was cold, like the one in my dream, but quieter, sadder. That had been a kiss of passion. This was a kiss of farewell.

That was the last time I saw them.

I was weeping. I didn't want to stay there beside the grave, so I scrambled up the hill behind the cemetery and sat down at the edge of the cliff, my tears blurring the distant line of the sea, which had retreated since Windy's time, after the river changed its course.

I didn't know why I was crying, exactly. Excitement, disappointment. Endings. Emptiness.

Windy and Phinny had found their lost child, but my family hadn't. My sister was still lost, more lost than ever, and in some ways so was I. Where did I belong? In my parents' long-gone house, where my feet knew every inch of the floor? In this tall, uncomfortable mansion, with my strange new friends straight out of some gothic novel? In the arms of a vanished ghost who loved a vanished ghost who wasn't me? Nowhere at all?

Someone sat down beside me. "Hey, Spooky. Don't cry. It's okay." It was Cole. "We'll figure out some way to help your parents, even without the treasure."

"That's not what I'm crying about," I said.

"What is it, then?"

"I don't know. It's just all so sad."

"The baby, you mean? Yes. But it was hundreds of years ago. He would be dead by now anyway."

"No, just . . . the whole sad story. Everything's so empty. Even the ghosts are dead. Windy and Phinny . . . they're gone now."

Cole put his arm around my shoulder. "Hey, *I'm* here. If this was a real Laetitia Flint novel, you know how it would end? With the two of us breaking the curse by marrying each other. I bet that's how she would have ended *Pirate Toogood's Treasure*, if she'd ever finished it—with a descendant of the Thornes marrying a descendent of the Toogoods."

"Are you asking me to marry you or something?"

He laughed. "I think we're a little young for that, don't you, Spooky? But admit it. You've always been crazy about me."

"Me? You?!" I looked at him. I saw the bully's best friend who had made my life miserable for a while. I saw the not-so-bad guy who had spent the past few weeks persistently making himself into my friend. And I saw the silky black hair, high cheekbones, and urgent eyes of his ancestor, Pirate Phineas Toogood.

He leaned forward and kissed me.

It wasn't a cold kiss, like Phineas's. It was warm and soft and *real*—and that made it scary. My first living kiss.

Then suddenly it was over.

With a scream I'd never heard her make before, living or dead, my sister came plummeting toward us like a train off its rails. The cliff edge gave way under Cole, and he fell.

CHAPTER TWENTY-EIGHT

Setting Kitty Free

I screamed too, I'm not sure what. "Help!" or "Cole!" or "Kitty!" maybe—or something incoherent.

Whatever it was, someone heard it. Two figures streaked out from behind me and plunged over the cliff after Cole. They reached him just seconds before he crashed on the rocks.

I lay at the edge of the cliff, staring down and trying to make sense of what I was seeing. Andre and Griffin were holding Cole between them in midair, lowering him to the ground. Andre was riding a broomstick—he must have grabbed Jonathan's—and Griffin . . . Griffin, it seemed, had wings.

My sister was still screaming overhead, but someone was screaming back at her in a voice that somehow overshadowed hers. It was me. "Kitty, go! Just GO!"

For a moment I thought she would bring the cliff down under me too—would bring the house down, and all the trees, and the hills, and the graves, and the whole planet. I braced myself for the fall. But instead, like a sound that gets higher and higher without getting any softer, until it's too high to hear, Kitty disappeared.

I lay shaking, my cheek pressed into the grass.

"Sukie, it's okay. Cole's safe. You're okay." Elizabeth kneeled beside me.

I curled on my side and sat up.

"We're all safe, for now," said Dr. Rust. "But, listen, Sukie. You have to do something about your sister. She'll be back, and she's too dangerous."

"But how? I can't control her! She never did anything like that before—she's getting worse and worse."

"I know. You're growing, and she can't. Ghosts hate that."

"And she was summoned with hell-smoke, back on Broken Isle, which can't have helped," said Elizabeth.

The hell-smoke—that must be what gave Kitty that scream, and that awful strength. She'd been getting angrier for months before it, though. Stronger, and less human. "But what can I *do*?"

"You have a way to summon her, don't you?" asked Dr. Rust.

"Yes, she gave me her whistle. She promised to come whenever I blew it. She promised to protect me."

"Call her, then, and release her from her promise."

"You're the only one who can," said Elizabeth.

"The sooner, the better," said Dr. Rust. "Do it now. We'll wait for you by Windy's grave."

I sat on a rock and stared at the horizon where Kitty had disappeared. I saw her in my mind's eye at the top of our hill, her red curls flying out as she spun around for an impatient moment to call, "Hurry up, Sukie!"

I remembered the watermelon smell of her favorite soap and how, when I came in from playing in the dirt, she would pull me to the bathroom and lather my hands under the cold tap. Then I would smell like Kitty for a little while.

I remembered sharing a bedroom with Kitty when we were really little. After Mom had kissed us good night and shut the door, I would beg her in whispers to read to me until at last Kitty would hiss, "All right, but just this once." We would climb out of our twin beds to kneel by the window, and she would murmur the words of whatever picture book was my favorite that week, turning the pages by the light of the orange streetlight, while I stumbled along, part reading, part remembering.

I remembered wrenching myself out of nightmares to crawl into her bed. "Ice-cube feet," she would mutter, but she would pull the blanket around me and fold me into her arms.

I remembered her freckles. I remembered the sunset on her hair, that red-orange color I had never seen since.

I remembered the emptiness after she died—the emptiness of the whole world and every individual thing in it.

I put the whistle to my lips and blew.

A film of the hell-smoke clung to the whistle. It tasted like death. Its sound was no longer my sister's urgent and familiar proxy, but a scream of pain.

Kitty answered the whistle, darkening the air. She had become a jagged shape with eyes the flame-red of her hair.

"Kitty," I said, "I'm sorry. I love you. I love you so much! But you have to go now."

She couldn't, she told me. I was letting myself get drawn into danger. She had to protect me. Evil people were threatening me. They were hurting me!

"They aren't hurting me. They aren't evil," I told her. I didn't add, *But you are, now.* "They're my friends. You have to stop!"

She couldn't. She had promised to protect me.

"I release you from your promise."

The edges of her shape jittered like dark lightning.

"I release you. I don't need you to protect me. I can take care of myself." I was crying now, choking on the words. "I love you, Kitty, but I don't need you anymore."

The sky went dark, and I couldn't breathe. I put the whistle on the rock beside me, picked up a jagged stone, and smashed it down.

Shards of bright blue plastic flew in all directions. The hard little ball from inside the whistle lay on the stone, shining like a drop of mercury. It grew brighter and brighter until it devoured my vision, and for a long moment, it was all I could see.

Then, quietly, it blinked out. The air cleared, and the day came back: fillips of wind, high clouds, bare trees, crows squabbling like siblings. I reached out to touch the little ball, but it wasn't there.

Neither was my sister, and I knew she never would be again.

CHAPTER TWENTY-NINE

My True Self

Back at the house, Cousin Hepzibah explained her plan. "The New-York Circulating Material Repository has offered to take this house on a long-term loan. I'm going to sell the land to that unpleasant real-estate man and use some of the money to build a new house—or rather, hire your father to build it. Your family can live there and take care of it for me, and I'll leave it to you in my will."

"Will you live there with us?"

She shook her head. "No, I'm staying in the Thorne Mansion for as long as I live. Longer, probably, if our ancestors are any indication."

"In the Poe Annex, you mean?"

"That's right. I like it there. It reminds me of my childhood."

"But will you be okay there, all alone?" I couldn't imagine explaining about the Poe Annex to my parents. But without Mom, who would help Cousin Hepzibah get dressed and navigate the stairs?

"Don't worry, I won't be alone," said Cousin Hepzibah.

"Several of the retired repositorians live in the annex. I met a very nice man there, Stan Mauskopf—he was Elizabeth's high school teacher. He's close friends with Griffin. He's been living in one of the Henry James houses."

"But who will help you with your bath and keeping the house clean?"

"Elizabeth is lending me some elves from the Grimm Collection. They like old houses, and they love housework. It will be fun."

That sounded all right. "I'll miss you so much! Will the Thorne Mansion stay in the Poe Annex forever?" It hurt to think of losing it along with her. The Thornes were my family, too—it was my ancestral home, just like hers. But I understood. The mansion was falling apart, and none of us could afford to keep it up.

"That's up to you," said Cousin Hepzibah. "I'm lending it to the repository for the rest of my life. It's yours after that—you can decide what to do with it then. You'll come visit me there, won't you?"

"Of course! All the time. It will be a good excuse to use the family broom."

"Good." She squeezed my hand with her thin, cold hand and smiled her birch-tree smile.

"Thank you, Cousin Hepzibah! A new house—I can't even believe it! I don't know what we would do without you."

"Or what *I* would do without *you*. It's a great relief to me to have found a true Thorne before I'm a ghost myself."

"Do you think you will be? A ghost, I mean. The house

feels a little empty without its ghosts." My sister certainly was gone. I hadn't felt anyone over my shoulder since I'd smashed the whistle. The emptiness was almost eerie.

Cousin Hepzibah smiled wryly. "Yes, I miss Windy and Phinny now that they're at peace. But they were never the only ghosts here. We'll just have to wait and see what happens. In any case, I promise you—" She stopped. "No, I think I won't make any post-animate promises after all."

"Good plan," I said. I had learned my lesson about ghosts making promises. "But, Cousin Hepzibah . . ."

"Yes, child?"

"Try to stick around for a while, okay?"

"I'll do my best."

I avoided Cole all that week. For once, he took the hint and left me alone on the bus. Maybe I should have worried that I'd lost a friend. But I couldn't make myself think about it. I didn't want to think about the two of us at all.

But I also couldn't *stop* thinking about the two of us.

Had that kiss been real, or only an echo of Phineas's kisses for Hepzibah Toogood? What had Cole meant by it? Were we just being controlled by the dead hand of Laetitia Flint, who had invented our ancestors?

Cole was right about one thing: If Flint had ever finished her novel, she would have made a Thorne girl marry a Toogood boy. Rereading the unfinished book, I had no trouble figuring out which ones, either: bland, simpering, virtuous Hepzibah Thorne—the 1840s Hepzibah—and kind, earnest, stout-hearted Robert Toogood, the pair who meet on the cliff walk, where the ghost of Japhet Thorne startles Hepzibah so that she almost tumbles to her death—except, luckily, Robert catches her.

That made me roll my eyes. Laetitia Flint couldn't get enough of ghosts startling people at the edges of cliffs.

But the manuscript stops short, before the couple has time to marry. And now here we were, me and Cole. Were we doomed to fulfill dead Laetitia's vision? Was that what Cole wanted? What about me—did *I* want that?

I sneaked a glance at Cole, who was sitting a few seats ahead of me on the bus, staring out the window with his back toward me. My sister was wrong about him—*had been* wrong about him, I corrected myself. Cole might be obnoxious, but underneath he was as kind and stout-hearted as any Flint hero. I liked him. And I'd liked that kiss.

But I hadn't thought of him that way, as someone you kiss. I hadn't really thought of *anyone* that way—anyone living, that is. If I had to pick, out of all the guys I knew, would I pick Cole? Over Andre, for example? Or all the guys I hadn't even met yet? Would I pick Cole over all of *them*? It was too soon to say.

When I got home—I'd started thinking of the Thorne Mansion as home, I noticed—Elizabeth Rew was in the parlor, drinking tea with Cousin Hepzibah.

"Come in, child," said my cousin. "Elizabeth and I were just discussing the arrangements for moving the house."

"Doc and I have been playing with ideas for more efficient ways to transport the annex buildings," said Elizabeth. "I thought maybe a jinni. Some of the jinn in *The Arabian Nights* can move palaces around by snapping their fingers. Like that palace in *Aladdin*."

"Aren't jinn hard to handle?" asked Cousin Hepzibah.

"Yes, they can be a pain—they hate going back into their lamps. Maybe we can borrow a nut instead. There's a hazelnut that holds a palace, in one of the German collections. Or was it a walnut in the Paris repository? I'll have to look into that."

"So Andre didn't come with you?" I asked.

"No, not this time. He has a chess meet."

I thought about asking Andre's advice about Cole. A year ago I might have asked my sister's advice. To my surprise, her loss no longer felt like a bitter wound—mostly I just felt wistful and relieved. My choices now really were my own.

A little while later, Cousin Hepzibah asked, "What do you think, child?"

"About what? I'm sorry—I was daydreaming," I said.

The old woman and the young one smiled at each other, as if I'd confirmed a joke between them. I blushed.

"Elizabeth," I asked, "you know that mirror you showed Feathertop? The one that showed him his true self?"

"Sure."

"Do you think . . . if I looked in it, would it show me *my* true self, too?"

"Try it and see." She hunted in her purse, took out a small mirror, and handed it to me.

I walked over to the window, where the afternoon sky was pearly-pink from the early spring sunset. I took a deep breath, squared my shoulders, and looked in the mirror.

The face I saw was different from how I imagined myself. The girl in the mirror looked older, more sure of herself. Both less weird and, paradoxically, less average. Not everyone might consider her attractive, I thought, with her long face and light eyebrows and lashes, but some people would. Most of all, she no longer looked doomed or damaged. That's what I'd always expected to see when I looked in the mirror, I realized, and what I'd always seen. I searched, but I couldn't find a trace of it now.

The future lay open in front of me, undecided, uncursed. Laetitia Flint may have meant to give my story a particular ending, but that didn't mean *I* had to.

I gave Elizabeth back her mirror. "Where is it from?" I asked.

"What, this? The El Dorado Pharmacy."

"What story is that in?"

"Hm? Oh, I see what you're asking. None—it's not fictional. It's just a mirror I bought in a drugstore near home."

How was that possible? "So that wasn't my true self I was looking at?"

"Of course it was, child," said Cousin Hepzibah. "Who else's would it be?"

CHAPTER THIRTY

The Cursed Development

The next morning, I beckoned Cole over on the bus. "You've been avoiding me," I said. I noticed he was still wearing Phineas Toogood's ring. I slid over to make room for him.

He sat down beside me. "No, *you've* been avoiding *me*."

"Well, maybe. But I always did, and that never stopped you from pestering me before."

He smiled. "You're kind of hard to resist, Spooky."

"I'm really sorry about my sister," I said. "You don't have to worry. She's gone now."

"That's okay, Spooky. It wasn't that . . . I mean, your sister was scary, and she did push me off a cliff. But it's not about her. It's you. I guess I'm not sure what you want."

"I'm not, either. But now I want you to not avoid me," I said. "Deal?"

"Deal. Is that all you want?" He glanced at my hand, where I was wearing Windy's ring.

"Well, pirate treasure would be nice, but that's not going to happen."

Cole laughed. "Don't be too sure, Spooky. *Pirate Toogood's Treasure* can't be the only novel with pirate gold buried in it."

"You're right. Hey, want to come down to the repository with me this weekend? I bet Andre has some ideas about where to start looking. Maybe we can bring Lola and Amanda, too."

"Sure, but it's going to be hard to fit all four of us on one broomstick. I wonder if my family has any broomsticks, or anything else like that?"

"Maybe Cousin Hepzibah can help you find them, if you do," I said.

"Yes, or maybe we could borrow that flying carpet from the repository," said Cole.

"Good idea! We totally need to check out those other collections in the basement! I bet there's a ton of amazing stuff."

"You know, Spooky," said Cole, "I knew things were going to be interesting that day I sat next to you on the bus. You have to admit, I'm kind of a genius."

"You're kind of a lot of things, Cole, I'll give you credit for that. And you're right. I may have underestimated you just a little."

In the months after I said good-bye to Kitty, spring came early, and everything changed. Sometimes I can't believe I'm the same person I was a year ago.

I often go up to the top of Thorne Hill Road, where the old Thorne Mansion used to stand, to visit the grave of Windy, little Jack, and Phinny's left hand. It's peaceful up there, with the smell of the roses and the view of the water.

The developers have had a terrible time getting their resort off the ground: first permit problems, then union disputes, then a fire tore through the architect's office, destroying the blueprints. They're saying the project is cursed.

My parents rented an apartment over a laundromat in North Harbor for my family to stay in while Dad's building the new house. It feels strange living with Internet and central heating again. Sometimes ghostly tremors make the glasses click together in the kitchen cabinets, but it's only the big clothes dryers shaking the floor downstairs.

We haven't found any pirate treasure yet, but I was right—Andre has lots of good leads. Lola and Amanda Pereira are helping us look, too. At first Andre wasn't so crazy about us telling other kids about the repository, but Elizabeth brought them to meet Dr. Rust, who gave them some kind of test, which they passed. Now Amanda turns pink and giggles whenever she sees Andre. I think she has a crush.

The repositorians didn't use a jinni or a walnut to transport the Thorne Mansion to the Poe Annex after all. Instead, they opened a portal in the graveyard and used a machine Leo Novikov had built to sort of twist the mansion through it. I was worried all the walls and furniture would shatter into toothpicks, but I should have trusted the repositorians. Whenever I visit Cousin Hepzibah—not with Leo's machine, just the ordinary way, by flying down on a broomstick and passing through the creeping horror of the Lovecraft Corpus—the mansion stands as tall and crooked in the Poe Annex moonlight as if it's been there for three hundred years, with every table and hearthrug exactly where it should be. Even the crows are still there.

And sometimes, when I shut my eyes, I can almost feel a ghost of an echo of Kitty.

AUTHOR'S NOTE

Laetitia Flint exists (so far) only in this novel, and her books can be found only in libraries of fictional fiction. To read them, consult a spectral librarian.

My favorite spectral librarians are in the novel *Lilith*, by George Macdonald (Mr. Raven); various stories by Jorge Luis Borges, especially "The Library of Babel"; and "The Tractate Middoth," by M. R. James (Dr. Rant).

All the other authors and books mentioned in this story are real. If you read them, you'll find many beautiful descriptions, heart-pounding adventures, and chilling visions. You'll also encounter attitudes that may jar today's sensibilities. Supernatural fiction from the nineteenth and early twentieth centuries often reflected the writers' anxieties, especially about women and people from other cultures, in ways that can seem ugly and shocking today.

I hope that won't scare you off. There's a lot to be learned—about the past, the present, and ourselves—from reading books we don't agree with. Take them with a spoonful of salt, and remember that our own great-great-great-great-great-great-great-great-great-grandnieces and -grandnephews will probably need a dose of salt when they read our stories.

A few more details:

New York City's flea markets exist, though I moved them around and populated them with fictional characters. Some of the best markets are gone now, victims of the city's ravenous appetite for real estate. But perhaps new ones will spring up.

People often ask me why the New-York Circulating Material Repository has a hyphen in its name. That's how New York used to be spelled until about one hundred fifty years ago; the repository was founded when everyone hyphenated the city's name. The New-York Historical Society, a wonderful place to visit, still uses the hyphen too.

Readers sometimes ask me if the New-York Circulating Material Repository really exists. Not in this universe, as far as I know. If you ever find it, please tell me!

In case you do want to try reading the books referred to in this one, here's a not completely comprehensive list of the authors and their works. Except for Diana Wynne Jones's Chrestomanci series and C. S. Lewis's Chronicles of Narnia (both of which I highly recommend for readers of all ages), none of them were written for children, so younger readers who find them hard going may want to try again after a few years.

Willa Cather: Various short stories, including "Consequences" and "Paul's Case"

Robert W. Chambers: Stories from *The King in Yellow*, especially the title story

Charles W. Chesnutt: Stories from *The Conjure Woman*, especially "The Goophered Grapevine" and "Po' Sandy"

James Fenimore Cooper: Various novels, especially *The Red Rover* and *The Water-Witch*

Mary Wilkins Freeman: Various stories from *The Wind in the Rose-bush*, especially "The Southwest Chamber" and the title story

Nathaniel Hawthorne: Various novels, novellas, romances, and short stories, including "Beneath an Umbrella," "The Celestial Railroad," *Fanshawe*, "Feathertop," *The House of the Seven Gables*, "Peter Goldthwaite's Treasure," *The Scarlet Letter*, *Septimus Felton*, *Twice-Told Tales*, "Young Goodman Brown"

Washington Irving: Various tales, especially from *A History of New-York* and *The Sketch Book of Geoffrey Crayon, Gent.*

Henry James: Novellas and short stories, including *The Turn of the Screw*

H. P. Lovecraft: *The Necronomicon* and innumerable, unutterable other works

Thomas Moore: "The Flying Dutchman"

Edgar Allan Poe: *The Narrative of Arthur Gordon Pym of Nantucket* and many short stories, including "The Assignation," "The Cask of Amontillado," "The Fall of the House of Usher," "The Gold-Bug," "The Masque of the Red Death," and "The Pit and the Pendulum"

Sir Walter Scott: *Rokeby*

Harriet Beecher Stowe: *Uncle Tom's Cabin* and various short stories in *Oldtown Fireside Stories*, especially "The Ghost in the Cap'n Browne House," "Captain Kidd's Money," and "The Sullivan Looking Glass"

Edith Wharton: *Ethan Frome*; various short stories, especially from *Tales of Men and Ghosts*, including "Afterward" and "The Eyes"

Herman Melville: *Moby-Dick*

Tales from *The Arabian Nights*

Finally, the Poe Annex's Spectral Library contains (among many others) fictional books that appear in the following works:

Hilaire Belloc: *Cautionary Verses*

A. S. Byatt: *Possession*

George Eliot: *Middlemarch*

Diana Wynne Jones: The Chrestomanci series

C. S. Lewis: *The Silver Chair*, from the Chronicles of Narnia

Vladimir Nabokov: *Pale Fire*

ACKNOWLEDGMENTS

This book would not have had a ghost of a chance without the encouragement and advice of many generous friends, relatives, and colleagues: David Bacon, Sarah Banks, Mark Caldwell, Catherine Clarke, Liz Cross, Lisa Dierbeck, Cyril Emery, John Hart, Katherine Keenum, Ruth Landé, Josephine Lemann, Deborah Lutz, Anne Malcolm, Laura Miller, Laurie Muchnick, Alice Naude, Sharyn November, Marina Picciotto, David Prentiss, Maggie Robbins, Emily Saxl, Ted Shulman, Dee Smith, Andrew Solomon, Owen Thomas, Chelsea Wald, Howard Waldman, Jaime Wolf, Scott York.

I'm especially grateful to my first readers and warmest supporters: my husband, Andrew Nahem; my mother, Alix Kates Shulman; my sister-in-writing, Anna Christina Büchmann; my patient friend Tom Goodwillie; my brilliant editor, Nancy Paulsen; and my incomparable agent, Irene Skolnick.

I would also like to thank the ghost of my father, Martin Shulman. Dad may not have had much use for stories about magic, but he loved long yarns about sailing ships, pirate treasure, and adventure on the high seas.

PRAISE FOR

THE GRIMM LEGACY

Bank Street Best Book
ALA Best Book for Young Adults
IRA Children's Choices
Mythopoeic Award finalist
School Library Journal Best Book
Nominated for numerous state awards (TN, TX, GA, VT, PA, MO, AR, CT, OK, MD, RI, SC, OR, SD)
Finalist for le Grand Prix de l'Imaginaire and nominated for le Prix Elbakin (French fantasy awards)

"A fizzy confection . . . the story buzzes along at a delightful clip."—*The New York Times Book Review*

★ "This modern fantasy has intrigue, adventure, and romance, and the magical aspects of the tale are both clever and intricately woven. . . . Fast paced, filled with humor, and peopled with characters who are either true to life or delightfully bizarre. Fans of fairy tales in general and Grimm stories in particular will delight in the author's frequent literary references, and fantasy lovers will feel very much at home in this tale that pulls out all the stops."—*School Library Journal*, starred review

"Captivating magic fills the pages. . . . Action fans will find plenty of heart-pounding, fantastical escapades as the novel builds to its satisfying, romantic conclusion. A richly imagined adventure with easy appeal for Harry Potter fans."—*Booklist*

PRAISE FOR

THE WELLS BEQUEST

Pennsylvania Keystone to Reading Middle School Book Award
Newsday Summer Reading Pick

★ "Hilarious time-travel dialogue. . . . A clever, sparky adventure made of science fiction, philosophy and humor."—*Kirkus Reviews*, starred review

"The inside-out plot construction is ably handled, with plenty of book-geek discursions . . . will draw readers into the science-fiction-made-real landscape."—*The Horn Book*

"Shulman once again crafts a marvelously engaging story that will have fantasy and sci-fi readers hooked. . . . The adventure, danger, and hints of romance will have readers swiftly turning pages, anxious to discover each new surprise."—*School Library Journal*

"A fun science fantasy adventure for all ages."—*Locus* magazine

"A madcap adventure story with plenty of danger and mystery thrown in."—*School Librarian*

"Full of . . . thought-provoking conundrums about the nature of time and reality, this is a stimulating story for imaginative readers."—*Carousel: The Guide to Children's Books*

"Absorbing, fast-paced sci-fi fantasy . . . five stars."—Common Sense Media